Cecily had been ten when Aunt Gin let her have a taste of beer one late summer afternoon.

They were sitting in lawn chairs in her aunt's big backyard beneath a tall maple tree, the wide, dense leaves keeping the sun off their skin. The air was hot and dusty dry without a whiff of breeze to cool things off, and Aunt Gin was fanning herself with a fancy fold-out fan she let Cecily play with sometimes.

Cecily thought the beer tasted gross, but because she knew it was something kids weren't supposed to have, she asked if she could have her own glass.

Aunt Gin laughed. "Oh, my, but you're going to get me in trouble with your mother. Viv will never forgive me for sending her daughter home with a taste for beer." Her eyes twinkling with amusement, she gave Cecily a long look. "You don't really like it, do you?"

Cecily scrunched up her nose. "No." She handed the beer back. "How come you do?"

"Can I tell you a secret?"

Cecily nodded. She was pretty good with keeping secrets. She didn't tell on Jimmy Cuthbert when he put an ice cube down Marilyn Skinner's dress because Marilyn Skinner had called Jimmy a turd. Of course, Cecily didn't like Marilyn Skinner either because she made fun of Cecily's name. But still, she knew she could keep one of Aunt Gin's secrets.

"The bunnies like it," Aunt Gin said.

from "Chance of Bunnies With Occasional Toad"

New Pages

a collection

ANNIE REED

TVp

Thunder Valley Press

New Pages

"Introduction" by Annie Reed, Copyright January, 2014

"The Shape of a Name" by Annie Reed, first published in Fiction River: How to Save the World, 2013

"Chance of Bunnies with Occasional Toad" by Annie Reed, Copyright 2012

"First Steps" by Annie Reed, Copyright 2012

"Another Door" by Annie Reed, Copyright 2012

"Night Passage" by Annie Reed, Copyright 2011

"Essy and the Christmas Kitten" by Annie Reed, Copyright 2010

"Love Among the Llamas" by Annie Reed, Copyright 2011

"Names in the Sand" by Annie Reed, Copyright 2011

Published by Thunder Valley Press
www.thundervalleypress.com

Cover art copyright © darrenmbaker/Bigstock.com
Book and cover design copyright © Thunder Valley Press

ISBN: 0615917267
ISBN-13: 978-0615917269

For more information on the author, go to www.annie-reed.com.

New Pages
a collection

ANNIE REED

Contents

Introduction   11

The Shape of a Name   13

Chance of Bunnies with Occasional Toad   35

First Steps   53

Another Door   69

Night Passage   85

Essy and the Christmas Kitten   97

Love Among the Llamas   113

Names in the Sand   125

Extras   137

INTRODUCTION

I love the experience of opening a new book. Whether I'm holding a paper book in my hands, feeling the crisp pages beneath my fingertips, or opening an electronic book on my e-reader, the program automatically taking me to the very first page, the excitement, the anticipation of starting a new book remains the same. Where will this one take me? Will I read with one eye open, turning the pages as quickly as I can to make sure everything turns out all right, or will I savor each word, luxuriate in the pictures the pages paint in my mind, reluctant for the book to end?

I never know until I turn that first new page.

For the women you're about to meet in the stories in this collection, life has taken a sudden, sometimes unexpected left turn. From a little girl orphaned in the war in Afghanistan to a widow learning to cope with life on her own to the woman who discovers an unexpected chance at love in the unlikeliest of places, each of these women is about to turn a new page in the book of her life. Their stories are sometimes harrowing, sometimes magical, but these women all have one thing in common—the kind of courage that gives women everywhere the ability to face adversity head on and come out stronger on the other side.

I hope you enjoy reading their stories as much as I enjoyed writing them.

—Annie Reed
Reno, Nevada
January 13, 2014

THE SHAPE OF A NAME

2007

Anoosheh never knew why the woman chose her.

The woman was beautiful and smelled clean like soap. One day she came to the tent where Anoosheh lived with the rest of the orphans who had lost arms or feet or legs. She wore strange clothes, and her *hijab* only covered part of her hair. No one in the refugee camp had hair the color of the setting sun like this woman did, and Anoosheh couldn't stop looking at it. Her own hair was dull and brown and dirty.

The woman spoke to all the children in the tent in a language Anoosheh didn't understand. When she came to the blanket where Anoosheh sat, the nurse told her Anoosheh's name. The woman sat down on the blanket next to Anoosheh and said something to her.

"She says your name means 'lucky,' and she asks if you know that," the nurse said.

Was she lucky? Outside her tent, men and women and older boys who still had their legs crowded around one of the trucks that brought supplies to the camp from Kabul. They pushed and shoved each other, trying to get food to feed themselves and their families. Those who didn't get a bag fought with the ones who did, grabbing the heavy bags from those too weak to protect what they had been given. Anoosheh had no parents, but men from the trucks always brought a bag of rice to the nurse along with new bandages, and another man stood guard over the tent so no one could take the children's food. She had never thought of herself as lucky, but she ate every day and had a blanket to sleep on at night, and the guard always crushed the scorpions he found in the tent under the heel of his boot, so maybe that meant her name was true.

When Anoosheh nodded, the woman smiled at her. Anoosheh started to smile back, but when the woman glanced at the bandage-covered stump where Anoosheh's hand used to be, the little girl blushed with shame and tried to hide her arm beneath the blanket.

She was older than her friend Hasti, who had lost both her arms when she tried to pick up a shiny toy in the street. Hasti still laughed and smiled when someone fed her or told her stories, or even when someone looked at the ragged stumps where her arms had been. Anoosheh couldn't smile like Hasti when people looked at her arm with its missing hand. She always wondered if people thought she was a thief. Anoosheh never stole, not even after her father left home to find work and didn't come back, and her family went hungry because her mother had to stay home to care for her new baby sister. Anoosheh had never tried to pick up a shiny toy in the street, but her hand was still gone.

She felt it sometimes, and she missed it always. It had been the hand she'd used to hold things and to write her name. Her mother had taught Anoosheh to write her name. You must be able to tell people who you are, her mother said. Your name is all people have to remember you by after you are gone.

Anoosheh had taught herself to write her mother's name. Setara, not *Madar Anoosheh*, as Anoosheh's father had called her mother. The shape of her mother's name was beautiful. After she lost her hand,

Anoosheh had practiced writing with her other hand, but the words always came out ugly.

"The nurse tells me you can write your name," the woman with hair the color of the sunset said. "Can you show me?"

The nurse told Anoosheh what the woman said, nodding at Anoosheh to let her know it was all right to do what the woman asked.

Anoosheh leaned forward and smoothed a spot on the dusty ground next to the blanket. Using a finger, she wrote her name and then her mother's in the dirt.

The words were still ugly. Anoosheh wanted her mother's name to be as beautiful as her mother had been, before the angry men beat her because her ankles were uncovered.

The woman leaned forward and smoothed the dirt, then wrote another word with her finger next to the ones Anoosheh had written. "Do you know this word?" she asked, speaking words that Anoosheh could understand.

Anoosheh had seen that word on a building in the city before her mother took Anoosheh and her baby sister and left their house to find a better place to live. Children had gone inside that building every day. Anoosheh had asked if she could go, but her mother always said Anoosheh wasn't old enough.

"School," Anoosheh said.

The woman didn't smile this time. Instead she asked Anoosheh, "How old are you?"

"Six," Anoosheh said.

The woman looked at the nurse and said something in the language Anoosheh didn't understand. Both women looked back at Anoosheh, and she felt her cheeks burn under the intensity of their stares.

When the woman left camp that afternoon, she took Anoosheh with her.

Anoosheh only had time to say a brief goodbye to Hasti.

Anoosheh helped the nurse feed Hasti sometimes, and she always told Hasti the same stories Anoosheh's mother had told her.

Hasti didn't want Anoosheh to go, she wanted another story, but Anoosheh had to say no, she didn't have time. The supply truck would be leaving soon, and Anoosheh and the sunset-haired woman would be on it when it left. No one had asked Anoosheh if she wanted to go, and she didn't want to leave Hasti behind.

"Can Hasti come with us?" Anoosheh asked.

The sunset-haired woman shook her head no and put glasses on her face that hid her eyes. When they left the tent, she murmured something in the language Anoosheh couldn't understand.

Anoosheh remembered the sound of those words, just like she remembered Hasti sobbing and calling for Anoosheh to come back. She would hear words like that often in her life, said by many different people in many different places. Once she learned what the words meant, she understood the reason the woman with the sunset hair hid her eyes.

"We can't save them all," the woman said as they left the orphans' tent behind. "I'm so sorry. We just can't save them all."

2009

Mastana pulled Anoosheh's *shaylah* down on her forehead. "I can see your hair," she said. "You can't go out like that. Everyone is to look their best today."

Anoosheh tugged her shaylah back where she'd had it. The plain, white cloth covering her head and wrapped around her neck was rough, and it always made her forehead itch. She didn't want it to touch her skin, but the teachers at the Maidan Shar Girls School made the students wear their entire uniform, even the uncomfortable *shaylahs*, whenever they were in public.

Anoosheh didn't mind the rest of her uniform. The soft black folds of the *jilbāb* she wore to cover her body had plenty of room for

Anoosheh to hide the books she took to read after class was over. Students were supposed to leave them in the classroom, because the teachers said they had to last, but Anoosheh was careful. She was sure her teachers wouldn't mind if they found out she took them to the room she shared with Mastana and the other girls who lived at the school, but she didn't want to take the chance. If a student broke too many rules, she was sent away, and Anoosheh had nowhere else to go.

Mastana was older than Anoosheh, but they sat next to each other in class while they learned mathematics and history and geography, English and Dari and Pashto.

Mastana thought she could tell Anoosheh what to do, and for the most part, Anoosheh let her. She had only one leg and used a crutch to walk. She never asked Anoosheh how she lost her hand, and Anoosheh never asked her how she lost her leg. Anoosheh thought that was what made them friends. They lived at the school along with six other girls who had no parents and three of the teachers' helpers who had no homes.

Everyone was nervous about the man coming to visit the school today. His name was Sayd Farouq Durani, and their teacher said all students were to address him as Shaghelay Farouq. Their teacher said he was the man who made it possible for Anoosheh and the other children to go to school and have enough food to eat so they could spend their time learning and not begging in the street. She told the girls that he spoke English better than any of the teachers in the school, and they should be ready to answer in English whatever questions he asked. Anoosheh hoped he wouldn't ask her how she lost her hand.

Shaghelay Farouq didn't come to their classroom right away. By the time the door opened and he walked inside, Anoosheh was so nervous she had trouble sitting still. Mastana had already pinched her once beneath the desk to make her stop wriggling.

Anoosheh had seen few men since she'd been taken from the

refugee camp by the woman with the sunset hair. Anoosheh hadn't seen her again, but now that she was learning English, she knew that was the language the woman had spoken. Anoosheh expected Shaghelay Farouq would have sunset-colored hair, too, because the teacher said he spoke such good English. She was surprised that he looked just like everyone else at Maidan Shar, only his face wasn't as hollow and his teeth were straight and white.

"Good morning, girls," he said in English.

Their teacher nodded. "Good morning, Shaghelay Farouq," all the girls in Anoosheh's class said in unison.

He looked at the students as if he wanted to remember all their faces. He paused when he reached Anoosheh, then his gaze moved on to Mastana. When he was finished, he sat down at the teacher's desk.

"For today," he said, "I want you to speak to me only in English, and you must use only the English form of address. You have been taught how to do that?"

Anoosheh sat very still. The teacher hadn't told them how to address someone like Shaghelay Farouq in English, and it hadn't been in any of the books she'd read.

When none of the students answered him, Shaghelay Farouq turned toward the teacher, who shook her head and looked as nervous as Anoosheh felt.

"Ah," he said. "Good. Now I can be useful. I was afraid you had already been taught everything you need to know." He smiled. "When I speak this language," he said in Pashto, "I am Shaghelay Farouq. But when I speak like this," he said in English, "I am Mister Durani. Please repeat that."

All the girls did, although none of them said the first word well.

"Very good," he said. "When I was much younger, I lived in Kabul until my work took me to the United States." He looked at Anoosheh. "Do you know where those places are?"

Her stomach clenched, but she nodded. She knew the names of

many of the places on the maps hung on the walls at the front of the classroom.

"Come up and show me," he said.

Anoosheh did as she was told. The classroom was small, the desks crowded together, and Anoosheh had to squeeze past Mastana, who sat on the outside of the row so she had a place to keep her crutch.

When Anoosheh got to the front of the class, she pointed to Kabul on the map of Afghanistan, then went to the map that showed the United States.

"Very good," he said. "I live in a state called Virginia. Can you show me where that is?"

She pointed to Virginia on the map of the United States before she realized that was something she'd learned by reading her geography book in her room. She saw Mastana's eyes grow as wide as her own must have been. Mastana knew that Anoosheh read at night before they had to turn out the light in their room.

Anoosheh froze. She expected Shaghelay Farouq—*Mister* Durani—to yell, or at the very least to strike her for disobeying the rules. She closed her eyes as he stood up from the desk, but no blow came.

"I would like you to come with me," he said to her instead. "I want to show you something you might enjoy. Something I believe you may be very good at. Would you like that?"

He wasn't angry with her? Maybe he thought all the students knew the names of the provinces in the United States.

Anoosheh realized he was waiting for her to answer. No one had ever asked her what she wanted to do.

"Yes," Anoosheh said. She couldn't say no to the man who made it possible for her to live at the school.

Mister Durani's smile widened. "Very good." He turned to the rest of the class. "Continue with your work. I will be back later, and perhaps someone can read to me from one of your lessons."

He held the door open for Anoosheh, and then he led her down the hallway toward a part of the school she had never seen.

"Your teacher tells me you are very bright, Anoosheh," Mister Durani said. "She says you read all the time, even when you should be sleeping."

Her teacher knew—and she'd told Mister Durani! Anoosheh bowed her head and waited for him to tell her she must leave the school. She would have to beg for food and find somewhere to sleep. The girls who lived outside the school with their families told stories of how they used to beg on the street, and how they had to run and hide from people who tried to hurt them.

Anoosheh didn't want to live like that. Why had she broken the rules?

"I'm very sorry," Anoosheh said softly. "I know I shouldn't have taken books from my classroom."

"I wish we had enough money to buy you even more books," he said. "Funds are limited, and we do what we can for as many as we can. Now, come see what I brought you here to show you."

He held the door open to a room filled with desks the size of her teacher's. Women sat working at machines Anoosheh had never seen before. Some seemed to be feeding fabric to the machines. Others moved their fingers over parts of the machine marked with letters.

One of the women in the room was a teacher's helper who lived at the school. She gestured for Anoosheh to come stand by her desk.

"This is a computer," she said, pointing at a machine on her desk. "I'm going to teach you to use it. We have limited access to the Internet here, but I'm going to teach you how to find places where you can read more books than you could possibly read in a lifetime."

Anoosheh didn't understand. How could something as small as this machine hold more books than she could read in her lifetime?

"Someday we hope to have enough computers for every student in the school," Mister Durani said. "Until then, we must start small." He smiled at her again. "In Maidan Shar, we're starting with you."

2014

The American soldiers were leaving Afghanistan.

Anoosheh didn't venture outside the school often. The streets weren't safe for girls her age. When she did go outside, it was impossible to go anywhere and not see an American soldier. Some of the soldiers were even women. They dressed in the same uniforms as the men and carried the same weapons, and they didn't have to cover their hair with a *hijab* when they were in public.

She didn't understand why a woman would want such a dangerous job. On the last field trip her class had taken with Mr. Durani to the school in Paghman, men on the street had hurled insults at the women soldiers, even though the women carried guns and the men didn't. If the women soldiers had not carried weapons, Anoosheh knew the men would have beaten them for daring to bare their heads in public.

She had first learned of the school in Paghman when Mr. Durani had given her the task of writing reports for the website he used to raise funds for the foundation he'd started that operated his two schools in Afghanistan. On one of his frequent visits, he'd told her the people who donated money to the foundation wanted to know who they were helping. Anoosheh was to be the public face of the Maidan Shar Girls School.

That had been two years ago, and Anoosheh had written many reports since then. She'd become very proficient at typing with her one hand and moving the mouse with the stump of her other arm. She still didn't like when people looked at the stump, but she'd learned to ignore their stares.

During his last trip to Maidan Shar, Mr. Durani had told her how he opened his first school in Kabul two decades ago. The school had accepted twenty boys out of the hundreds Mr. Durani had met in the Afghan refugee camps in Pakistan.

"The building was old and all I could afford," he'd said. "It did not last the first winter."

Anoosheh knew that Mr. Durani was not a wealthy man. He'd had no funds to rebuild or relocate the school, and he'd had to send the students away. He'd said that had been the hardest thing he'd ever done, even harder than leaving Afghanistan and moving his wife and children to the United States.

There he had started the foundation that now operated the Maidan Shar Girls School and the Paghman school for both boys and girls. He'd said he hoped to start another school soon, one that would teach children and young adults who'd lost limbs in the war useful skills so that they could earn a living.

There were so many children like Anoosheh and Mastana. And Hasti.

Anoosheh had used the computer to try to find out what had happened to Hasti. She'd used the computer to learn many things, and one thing she'd learned was that the world was much larger than Wardak province or Afghanistan or even the Middle East. In a world that big, it was easy to forget one small, armless girl.

It looked like the world had forgotten Hasti, because Anoosheh hadn't been able to find any mention of her anywhere.

Anoosheh didn't know what would happen after the American soldiers went home. She'd read much about the history of her country, and she knew more than what was in the approved textbooks the teachers used in class. Countries with bigger and better-equipped armies had invaded Afghanistan before. The American soldiers had been training the Afghan army, so perhaps the next army to invade would take its time. Anoosheh hoped so. Her country was struggling, and so were many of its citizens.

Mr. Durani told her once that she was very adult for someone so young, always thinking of such serious things. Anoosheh didn't tell him that she hadn't really been a child since her mother and baby sister had been killed in front of her by a man who'd become angry because her mother had refused him. Anoosheh had screamed at him and hit him, and he'd smashed her hand with his gun over and over again until her flesh tore away from her bones. If another man on the way to the refugee camp hadn't found her, wrapped a tourniquet around her bleeding arm, and carried her to the medical tent, where doctors had amputated what was left of her ruined hand, she would have died on the road next to her mother and sister.

When the teacher's assistant at the back of the work room shrieked, Anoosheh had just started writing her latest report on the computer. The school had more computers now that the students could use, but Anoosheh had always preferred the one in the assistants' room.

None of the assistants stared at her while she worked. Now they all stared wide-eyed, their work forgotten, as the assistant stopped shrieking and began to sob.

"What is it, Nurani?" one of the other assistants asked. "What is wrong?"

Nurani pointed at the screen of her computer. Tears ran down her cheeks. "He's dead. Mr. Durani is dead!"

Anoosheh went very still as a cold, hard feeling settled in her chest. The feeling radiated down her arms into her fingers, even the fingers of the phantom hand she rarely felt anymore.

"How?" someone asked.

Nurani shook her head, unable to speak.

Another assistant, her face pale with shock, went over to comfort her. She read what was on Nurani's screen. "The email says men came to the school in Paghman while Mr. Durani was there visiting. The men wanted to take girls who did not belong to them. Mr. Durani tried to stop them. One of the men shot him, and they all ran away." She looked up from the computer, and her eyes met Anoosheh's. "His daughter sent this email to every assistant and teacher, and to you, Anoosheh."

Anoosheh looked at the icon on the bottom of her computer screen. She'd been so intent on her report that she hadn't noticed when the icon indicated she had an email waiting. Now she didn't want to open it. She didn't want to read the words herself. The shape of those words would be ugly.

One by one, the teachers told all their classes that Mr. Durani had died, and then the students were dismissed for the day. Anoosheh and Mastana still lived at the school, only now they cared for the younger girls who had no families to go home to. Not all of the girls knew Mr. Durani, and Anoosheh had to explain why everyone was so sad.

That night, after the younger girls had fallen asleep, Mastana came to sit next to Anoosheh on her narrow bed. Mastana still walked with a crutch. If she was jealous of the attention that Anoosheh had gotten from Mr. Durani over the years or the things Anoosheh had been taught outside the classroom, she'd never said anything.

"What will happen to us now?" Mastana asked. "Without Mr. Durani, will the school continue?"

Anoosheh knew Mastana hoped to remain with the school as a teacher, just as Anoosheh wanted to stay and continue her work on behalf of the schools. She also knew that Mr. Durani did not run his foundation alone. He had people who helped him, although those people never came with Mr. Durani when he visited Afghanistan.

"It will be all right," Anoosheh told Mastana. "The schools are too important to too many of us. The people who are left will find a way to keep them open."

Mastana nodded and hugged her tight. Anoosheh returned the hug, and for the first time that day, allowed herself to cry. She told herself she was crying for Mr. Durani, but she knew some of her tears were for herself and the friend she had just lied to and the orphaned girls in this room.

Anoosheh had learned too much working on the computer. One thing she knew for certain was that compared to the vastness of the entire world, one little school like Maidan Shar was not very important at all.

2026

Anoosheh didn't like Kabul. There were too many people and too much noise, and even through the fabric of her *burqa*, the city smelled of cars and unwashed bodies and fear.

Not that Anoosheh saw much of the city. The *burqa* she had to wear in Kabul covered her head to toe. Although the cloth was lightweight, it made her feel claustrophobic. Only a small cutout over her eyes let her see the world, and even that was covered by mesh that made everything look hazy and indistinct.

She remembered when she used to hate wearing the *shaylah* when she'd been a student at the Maidan Shar school. She didn't know how lucky she'd been back then. The only good thing about being forced to wear a *burqa* was that the fabric hid her anger.

The schools that had played such an important part in her life were in trouble. Schools for children from the refugee camps were not popular with all segments of Afghan society, and the schools run by the foundation established by Mr. Durani were the least popular of all. The curriculum at his schools did not come solely from textbooks approved by the Ministry of Education, but from a wide-ranging variety of sources Anoosheh had helped develop since she'd been appointed to the board of what was now The Sayd Farouq Durani Children's Foundation.

The entire curriculum had come under scrutiny by the Ministry of Education, and representatives from the board had been summoned to Kabul to meet with a representative of the Ministry to discuss the Ministry's findings, as if well-educated and adequately-fed bureaucrats knew the best way to educate children who had been traumatized by war.

Anoosheh had never wanted to be on the board, but several years ago Mr. Durani's daughter, the one who had emailed the school about his death, had approached Anoosheh because she felt the American board members were too far removed from the children her father had devoted his life to helping. Anoosheh agreed. From her perspective, it had become clear in the years following his death that Mr. Durani had been the driving force of the foundation. Anoosheh had told Mr. Durani's daughter that she would serve on the board, such service to be conditioned on her continued employment by the schools. With the support of Mr. Durani's daughter, the vote to approve her had been unanimous.

Anoosheh did not underestimate the importance of today's meeting. The Ministry of Education could order the schools closed.

Even if the board had not decided Anoosheh should attend, she would have gone anyway, but as a single woman, she could not attend without a male member of the board. Oren Culbertson, a Texas oil millionaire, had been designated by the board to be the American face of the foundation at the meeting.

Only Mr. Culbertson was late.

Anoosheh sat primly in her chair and tried not to fidget. Perhaps in an attempt to impress the rich American, the Ministry of Education had arranged to use a spacious conference room on the third floor of a new office building in downtown Kabul. The furniture was made of steel and glass and black leather, and the large windows overlooking downtown Kabul were bulletproof.

She wasn't worried about gunfire from the street. This decade's war centered in the north, the battles little more than border skirmishes. No violence had touched the capital city.

The fighting had the potential to be the first wave of the next invasion of her country, but she thought it unlikely. The would-be invaders had no support from the world's superpowers, and their belief in arcane religious dogma did not rise to the level of suicidal fervor. The only potential violence here was what the representative of the Ministry of Education who sat across the conference table from her could do to her schools. If the way he kept glancing at the clock on the wall was any indication, the outlook was not good.

When Mr. Culbertson finally arrived, he was not alone. He introduced the woman who accompanied him as his wife. Anoosheh stood and began to nod a polite greeting, then stopped when she realized she knew this woman.

Mrs. Culbertson was much older now, and the few strands of hair poking out from beneath the *hijab* she wore tight around her face were no longer the color of the setting sun. Still, she had no trouble recognizing the woman who'd taken her from the refugee camp after Anoosheh had written her mother's name in the dirt.

As Anoosheh feared, the meeting did not go well. Mr. Culbertson spouted well-rehearsed rhetoric about mission and empowerment and educational opportunities for the underprivileged in a manner which he no doubt felt was friendly—and it might have been in Texas—but here in Kabul his words only sounded disrespectful and condescending.

The representative from the Ministry of Education stayed silent and allowed Mr. Culbertson to continue to talk until it became clear even to Mr. Culbertson that he had nothing left to say. When he finally stopped talking, the representative, a small man who clearly relished his power over others, sat forward in his chair.

"Your schools do not teach the approved texts," he said. "How can you expect your students to integrate into Afghan society if they are not taught Afghani traditions?"

Anoosheh cleared her throat softly, hoping that Mr. Culbertson would hear and offer her the opportunity to speak.

He didn't, but his wife did. "I believe Anoosheh has something she would like to say," she told her husband. "Go ahead, dear," she said to Anoosheh in the same flawless Pashto she'd used in the camp. Anoosheh had never known why the woman had spoken English at all that day. Perhaps it had been a test to determine who could understand her.

"With all respect," Anoosheh said to the arrogant little man from the Ministry of Education. "Students who have been traumatized by violence should not be taught to merely integrate into Afghan society." Anoosheh knew well enough on what rung of Afghan

ANNIE REED

society the representative thought her students belonged. "They should be taught they can excel as well as any child."

The representative from the Ministry of Education turned his cold gaze on her. "I was told you are here because you teach at the school. This does not concern you."

"Anoosheh is a member of our board," Mr. Culbertson said to the minister. "She is also our school's brightest scholar, and a fine example of the success of our teaching methods. She was only six years old when she first came to our schools."

If Anoosheh hadn't been so angry, Mr. Culbertson's praise might have made her proud. As it was, she had a difficult time keeping her tone non-confrontational.

"With respect," she said again. "We teach the approved texts at the school, as the Ministry requires. We also teach our students how to integrate into the larger world in which they live. These are skills which the board believes will best serve our students and help them overcome the difficulties they will face as adults."

Even before she finished speaking, Anoosheh could tell that the cause was lost. The Ministry had made its decision before the meeting started.

The representative turned his attention back to Mr. Culbertson. "Your schools will begin teaching the approved texts, and only the approved texts, effective immediately. The Ministry will send representatives to the schools to observe all classes. Should any class be found in violation of this order, your schools will be shut down and the students returned to their families." He stood. "The decision is final."

Anoosheh was shaking by the time the representative left the room. Half the children in her schools had no families. If the schools closed, they would turn to begging on the streets.

She would have to find a way to keep teaching the children the things they needed to know to succeed in a world that included more than just Afghanistan, no matter how insular the Ministry wanted to make the education system. She had to make this work. She owed it to the students. She owed it to the memory of Mr. Durani. Mastana would help. Mastana was one of the best teachers at the Maidan Shar school.

"Anoosheh, can I have a minute?" Mr. Culbertson said, startling her. She'd been so deep in thought she had forgotten he was there.

Even through the mesh of her *burqa*, she could tell he was about to deliver more bad news.

"The board...well, they've asked me to relay a message to you," he said. "I'm afraid it's not very pleasant, so we should just get right to it." He cleared his throat, and then held himself up straighter. "The board wants to thank you for your years of service, but what with the way things are over here these days, the board feels it's better to play along and make sure the schools keep running. We realize you're passionate about your beliefs. We just don't think those beliefs are more important than keeping the schools going, even if all we do is give the kids a basic education and a hot meal every day."

Anoosheh couldn't believe this. "Are you telling me I'm no longer on the board?"

He spread his hands wide. "We'd also like you to resign from the school."

She recognized the gesture from the videos she'd watched on her computer. He was telling her it wasn't his fault, that he was doing the best he could. She wished she could believe him.

"Look, we're not saving the world here," he said. "We're just trying to keep these kids alive and teach them enough so they can stay that way."

"You're wrong," she said. She turned her body toward Mrs. Culbertson. "'We can't save them all,' that's what you said when you took me from the camp."

Mrs. Culbertson remembered. The look of shock on her face gave her away. "Yes, I did say that. It was the hardest lesson I've learned doing this work."

"But by saving me, you saved a small piece of the world," Anoosheh said. "When we help a child reach her best potential, you make that piece of the world better. Can't you see? We are saving the world. Making it a better place. That's all I've been trying to do. Make this world a better place for all children, not just the ones born of privilege."

Mrs. Culbertson's eyes grew moist, but she didn't cry. "I'm sorry, I truly am. The board's focus has to be on keeping the schools open. That means we have to play by the rules the Ministry sets for us."

"At least until the political climate over here shifts again," Mr. Culbertson said. "Then maybe we can revisit this decision."

Anoosheh closed her eyes and bowed her head. She could not believe Mr. Durani would have wanted this. He had introduced her to the world beyond the school when he allowed her to use the computer. He had given her a great gift that day, and she had worked the rest of her life trying to repay him by continuing the work he'd started. She had no intention of stopping now.

She straightened her spine and looked Mr. Culbertson in the eye through the hated mesh of her *burqa*. "I would like to start a new school," she said. "I would appreciate any assistance you can give me."

Mr. Culbertson shook his head. "I'm afraid that I can't do that, Anoosheh. I'm pretty sure you understand why."

Anoosheh rode down in the elevator with Mr. Culbertson and his wife so she wouldn't appear to leave the building unaccompanied, but she said nothing else to them.

Thanks to her position on the board of Mr. Durani's foundation, she knew that the money to operate his schools didn't all come from millionaires like Mr. Culbertson. People all around the world donated small amounts of money year after year to the foundation that bore his name. Anoosheh could start a new foundation of her own to do the same thing. It would take time for enough small donations to equal one new school, but Mr. Durani had made educating Afghan orphans like Anoosheh his life's work. Could she do anything less?

2041

The narrow road that hugged the mountains might have been paved at one time, but now it consisted of hard-packed dirt and rocks bordered on one side by a sheer drop off and the steep mountain face on the other. Anoosheh had made the mistake of looking out the side window of the transport into the ravine. The rusted-out carcasses of cars littering the ground far below gave silent witness to travelers who had not driven this road carefully enough. Anoosheh spent the rest of the trip giving silent thanks for her skilled driver.

The village at the end of this road was tucked into a narrow valley between the high mountain peaks. The village was little more than a gathering of flat-topped houses built against the mountain, and like many places in Afghanistan, had been the site of fierce fighting between the Afghan army and religious factions intent on imposing their will upon the entire country. The fighting was over now, and the villagers were rebuilding. The newest addition was the school sponsored by Anoosheh's foundation.

Mastana had tried to dissuade Anoosheh from traveling to the village for the school's dedication. Anoosheh's bones were not as strong as they'd once been. The doctors told her the malnutrition she'd suffered as a child had permanently damaged her. The fragility of her body prevented her from using new technology that could have given her a replacement hand that functioned like the hand she had lost, but by now Anoosheh had long since forgotten the shame she used to feel about her stump.

Anoosheh had her own dedication ceremony she wanted to conduct in private, as she had done for all sixteen schools her foundation had opened in villages like this one. It had taken her years to open the first school, but her foundation was self-sustaining now, thanks to donations from people the world over. The Ministry of Education chose to ignore her as long as she operated in remote regions of the country, and that suited Anoosheh. After all, she had never liked Kabul.

Her driver stopped the transport in front of her newest school. Anoosheh did not need to inspect the interior of the little house. It was divided into two simple classrooms, one for boys and the other for girls, like all her schools. Once the children learned basic skills, Anoosheh's foundation would pay to install the technology necessary to connect the school to the greater world beyond.

Anoosheh got out of the transport and made her way to the school's front door. As with all her schools, a flat stone plaque had been installed to the left of the door. Her driver brought the supplies she needed, and Anoosheh went to work with her brush.

First she painted her mother's name on the plaque, followed by her father's. Next she painted Sayd Farouq Durani's name. The last name she painted was Hasti, long gone now, but never forgotten.

As she finished, Anoosheh became aware that she'd drawn the interest of a small crowd of children. "Are you a teacher?" a small boy asked.

"I was." Anoosheh pointed at the names she'd written. "Can you write your name?"

The boy shook his head.

"You will learn," she said.

"Zeyba can write her name," the boy said.

A girl near the back blushed furiously and ducked her head. She wore no *hijab*, and she would wear no *shaylah* in Anoosheh's school.

"Come here," Anoosheh said to her. "Show me."

The girl did as she was told. She smoothed a place in the dirt and began to write with a finger, but Anoosheh stopped her. "Here," she said, handing the girl the brush. She pointed at the empty space at the bottom of the plaque. "Write your name here."

The girl's eyes widened. "My writing is bad. It will look ugly."

The shapes of the names Anoosheh had painted weren't as beautiful as the ones she'd written as a child before she'd lost her hand, but she'd come to realize over the years that beauty was in the memory, not the writing. As long as her schools existed, people would read the names of the people she cherished and would know that these people had once lived.

"Do you know why we write names?" Anoosheh asked the girl.

She shook her head.

"Names are how people remember you." Anoosheh smiled at her. "I wish to remember meeting you this day."

The girl looked dubious, but she painted her name at the bottom of the plaque. The driver would no doubt want to paint over the ragged letters before he sealed the stone, but Anoosheh wouldn't let him.

"What is your name?" the girl asked when she was done. "Did you write it here?"

"No." Anoosheh hadn't painted her name on any of her schools.

The girl handed her the brush. "I want to remember you."

Did she deserve to be remembered? Who was she to say? Perhaps this day would be as important to Zeyba as the day Mrs. Culbertson had come to the refugee camp had been for Anoosheh.

While Anoosheh painted her name, she considered Julia Culbertson. The woman was directly responsible for giving Anoosheh a chance to be more than a maimed orphan begging in the streets, yet she'd never included Julia's name on any of the plaques. Julia Culbertson had passed away in her sleep a year after she'd come to Kabul with her husband.

When Anoosheh finished writing her name, she painted another, only this time in English. Zeyba's life would be better because of what Julia Culbertson had done. She hadn't saved everyone, but like Mr. Durani, she'd saved far more than she knew. They may have focused on their failures, but Anoosheh preferred to remember their successes.

The world was changing because of their work. The world should remember the shape of their names.

CHANCE OF BUNNIES WITH OCCASIONAL TOAD

The house smelled dusty and abandoned.

Just like me, Cecily thought.

For a minute there, the old-fashioned lock, rusty with age, fought her. Cecily worried the real estate agent had given her the wrong key, but eventually the doorknob turned, and she pushed the door open.

Even though Cecily was a grown woman with a place of her own, it felt odd opening this door with a key that now belonged to her, just like the house itself now belonged to her. During all the summers when she'd been sent to live in this house with her aunt because her mother couldn't deal with having Cecily home from school for an entire three months, Cecily had never unlocked the door herself.

She could have. Cecily was one of a generation of "latch key" kids, a by-product of the feminist movement that saw women like her mother working nine-to-five jobs while their kids went to school from nine to three.

Cecily had worn her house key on a lanyard around her neck, and for two and a half hours every afternoon, she sat by herself at the dining room table and did her homework in an empty house. Not because she wanted to, but because her mom would check Cecily's work first thing, even before starting dinner, and if Cecily couldn't show her mom two and a half hours' worth of work, she was grounded from watching television for the night.

Her aunt didn't place the same restrictions on Cecily as her mom had.

"Summer is a time for fun," her aunt used to say. "To read because you want to. Eat in the living room, have dinner for breakfast or breakfast for dinner. It's not a time for kids to worry about keys. Keys are for grownups."

The front door opened directly into the living room. Cecily stepped inside and shut the front door behind herself.

The room looked both smaller and larger than she remembered. Smaller, she supposed, because the last summer she spent here, she was only twelve years old. If she ever went back to her elementary school, it would probably look smaller, too. Perspective changed with age, and right now, Cecily felt every single one of her thirty-three years.

God, had it been that long since she'd visited her aunt?

All her aunt's furniture was gone, which made the room look larger.

Cecily had handled those details over the phone. "Find a charity," she'd told her aunt's estate lawyer. "One that benefits abused women." She'd paused, remembering. "Or an animal rescue organization. I don't care about the write-off. Just make sure they can use my aunt's things, not just toss them away."

The real estate people had done a good job cleaning the inside of the house. Fresh, not-quite-white paint covered the walls. The old avocado-shaded nubby carpeting was spotless, if a little threadbare in places. She remembered stretching out on that carpet reading comic books, of all things. Her mom never let Cecily spend money on comics at home.

In place of her aunt's comfortable furniture, impersonal Pottery Barn knockoffs created a not quite lived-in look. A generic bookcase was centered on one wall, an uncomfortable, over-stuffed chair against another. Tasteful brochures from the realtor's office fanned out on a glass-topped coffee table. A silk flower arrangement crouched on the mantle over the brick fireplace, but the house felt empty.

Unlived in.

The sight of it all made Cecily ache. Her aunt was really gone. Maybe coming here had been a bad idea, but Cecily had to know. The adult she'd grown into wouldn't let her say goodbye to this part of her life without knowing.

A framed print of a watercolor landscape centered just so on the wall opposite the front door reflected Cecily's silhouette back at her. Just for a minute, she could almost see her aunt in that reflection, not as Cecily had last seen her—a jovial, round woman of indeterminate middle age; ancient, really, to a twelve-year-old—but as she must have been in the last years of her life. A little bent with age, her hair gone frizzy white and thin, but still with that broad grin on her face, the one that said life was far more fun that Cecily's mom would ever know.

That grin—that attitude—was the thing that Cecily treasured most about her Aunt Gin. It was the thing she didn't realize she would miss so badly after her aunt was gone.

"I could do all this for you," her mom had said. "Honestly, I don't know why Ginger wanted you to handle her estate. I'm her sister."

Cecily knew why, not that she could ever tell her mom. What could she say? "Because of the bunnies, Mom." Her mom would never understand.

Cecily was here for the bunnies.

Bunnies, and the occasional toad.

Cecily had been ten when Aunt Gin let her have a taste of beer one late summer afternoon.

They were sitting in lawn chairs in her aunt's big backyard beneath a tall maple tree, the wide, dense leaves keeping the sun off their skin. The air was hot and dusty dry without a whiff of breeze to cool things off, and Aunt Gin was fanning herself with a fancy fold-out fan she let Cecily play with sometimes.

Cecily thought the beer tasted gross, but because she knew it was something kids weren't supposed to have, she asked if she could have her own glass.

Aunt Gin laughed. "Oh, my, but you're going to get me in trouble with your mother. Viv will never forgive me for sending her daughter home with a taste for beer." Her eyes twinkling with amusement, she gave Cecily a long look. "You don't really like it, do you?"

Cecily scrunched up her nose. "No." She handed the beer back. "How come you do?"

"Can I tell you a secret?"

Cecily nodded. She was pretty good with keeping secrets. She didn't tell on Jimmy Cuthbert when he put an ice cube down Marilyn Skinner's dress because Marilyn Skinner had called Jimmy a turd. Of course, Cecily didn't like Marilyn Skinner either because she made fun of Cecily's name. But still, she knew she could keep one of Aunt Gin's secrets.

"The bunnies like it," Aunt Gin said.

"That's not a secret, that's just silly." Bunnies ate grass. They didn't drink beer.

"Occasionally the toads enjoy a nice cold beer on a hot day, too."

Aunt Gin was teasing her, she had to be. "Everyone knows toads eat flies," Cecily said. She hoped any toads that showed up in Aunt Gin's yard ate flies. A few persistent flies had been landing on her sweaty skin, and she'd grown tired of swatting at them. "Nasty old flies."

"They do eat flies," Aunt Gin said. "With a nice beer chaser. You ever taste a fly?"

Cecily shook her head.

"Well, compared to a fly, beer tastes pretty darn good."

Aunt Gin liked to tease, but not in a mean way like the kids at school. It was more like she enjoyed making things up. That's what Aunt Gin did for a living, her mom said. Made stuff up.

It wasn't until she was much older that Cecily realized her aunt was a writer. When she was ten, all she knew was that Aunt Gin would spend her nights typing in a little room off the hallway right behind the living room.

Sometimes her aunt pounded the keys on her old typewriter so fast, it sounded like the *rat-a-tat-tat* of gunfire on a television show, interrupted often with the ring of a little bell and the ratcheting sound of the carriage return. Other times, Aunt Gin would sit in that room with the door half-closed, listening to music on her record player, and not type a word.

But no matter how hard and fast her aunt typed or how late she stayed in that room each night, Aunt Gin always found time to spend with Cecily the next day. Even if that meant all they did was sit outside beneath the maple tree while Cecily read a comic book and Aunt Gin sipped a beer.

Cecily's friends back home thought spending a summer this way was boring, but she loved it, and not just because she got to do things with Aunt Gin she didn't get to do at home. Aunt Gin had a huge backyard dominated by that big maple tree. The lawn wasn't much, but flowers grew along the fence in between bushy shrubs, and there was a little pond with a fountain in one corner in the back.

Plastic statues and figurines, mostly of things like squirrels and chipmunks and birds and a silly-looking cat standing on his back legs, playing a violin, peeked out between the flowers and the shrubs. Cecily always had something to look at, and when she'd been little, things to play "let's pretend" with. She'd lost track of the number of times she'd whirled around in the yard, dancing to music the cat was playing just for her.

One side and the back of Aunt Gin's yard were closed off with a tall redwood fence, but the other side had only a little split-rail fence. On the other side of the split-rail fence was a field that seemed to go on forever.

"That's why I love this place," Aunt Gin had told her one time when they were sitting beneath the maple tree. "All that open space, as far as I care to see. There's magic in open spaces, you know. That's where imagination lives."

At ten, Cecily didn't know about magic, but she knew about the rabbits that lived in the fields. She saw them now and then, cute little brown bunnies with fluffy white tails. She told her aunt once that she wished she could hold one because it looked so soft and cuddly.

"You can't hold magic, Cici. If you try, it runs away. That's why adults can't see magic anymore. They want to own it. Control it. They've forgotten how to slow down and just let the magic happen."

Her aunt had been the only one who'd ever called her Cici. She'd liked it. Cici didn't sound nearly as odd as Cecily. Marilyn Skinner wouldn't make fun of a Cici.

It never occurred to Cecily back then that she could have decided she wanted everyone to call her Cici. Her mom told her Cecily was dignified, which was what a young lady should be. After she'd gone to law school, Cecily sounded more like what a lawyer should be called. Not Cici.

No, Cici had been the young girl who'd snuck out of her aunt's house in the middle of the night, beer in hand, to see if bunnies and toads really drank the bad-tasting stuff.

She'd poured the beer into a small bowl with short enough sides that she figured a bunny could reach. She wasn't sure about a toad, but she didn't really care about toads. It wasn't like she wanted to touch one. She really, *really* wanted to touch a bunny.

She'd sat in a lawn chair in her aunt's backyard all night, wrapped in a throw off her bed. Her aunt had the door to the typewriter room closed all the way, so it hadn't been that hard to sneak out. The stars filled the night sky. Cecily could hear the gentle burbling of the fountain and the buzzing of night insects. The yard was dark, but there was just enough light from the neighbors' house, where they kept their back door light on all night, it seemed, that Cecily could see the little bowl where she'd left the beer.

She wasn't trying to trap the bunnies. Really. She just wanted to see one up close, and she hoped that if she gave it the beer her aunt said it liked, it might let her touch it.

She thought she'd be able to stay awake all night. She hadn't been tired when she first went outside, but the throw was soft and thick and comfortable. She sometimes took naps in the lawn chair on a hot afternoon, and it really was a long night to just sit and wait. It wasn't surprising that before long she fell fast asleep.

When she woke up, the sky was just starting to get light with the first hint of dawn. Cecily hadn't meant to be outside all night long. Would her aunt be upset? Cecily's mom would be. Aunt Gin wasn't like her mom, but Cecily still didn't want to make her mad. Kids weren't supposed to sleep outside all night, especially not when they'd snuck out of the house to begin with.

Something rustled in the grass near the rail fence. Cecily held her breath as a rabbit hopped close to the bowl. The bunny was little more than a dark shape against the darker grass, but its fluffy white tail gave it away. The neighbors' back porch light made the bunny's dark eyes glisten.

The bunny hopped slowly, like Cecily knew bunnies did when they didn't feel threatened. She'd seen them freeze stock still in the field when they heard a dog or when they saw Cecily come out into the backyard. Then they'd hop away like crazy, their fluffy white tails bouncing along behind them.

The bunny got close to the bowl. Was it really going to drink the nasty old beer?

Something odd happened then. Something that Cici the ten-year-old thought might have been a dream, and something the adult Cecily thought was the result of straining too hard to see things in the dim light of early dawn and listening to too many of her aunt's stories.

A little pinprick of light fluttered out from one of the bushes near the back of Aunt Gin's yard. Another little light joined it, and then another and another until a whole group of little floating, fluttering lights drifted toward the bunny.

Cecily had seen fireflies before. These little lights were too small to be fireflies. Whatever they were, some of them settled on the top of the bunny's head, and others settled on the rim of the bowl.

Soon so many of the little fluttering things ringed the bowl that they made it look like one of those glow-in-the-dark stars Cecily's friend Crystal had on the ceiling of her bedroom.

Then the toad came.

Like the bunny, the toad hopped slowly across the grass from beneath a shrub near the split-rail fence. Unlike the bunny, the toad had a much larger glowing thing riding on its back. Cecily thought it looked like a butterfly.

She blinked her eyes, trying to see clearly. That simple movement made everything freeze. The bunny went still, just like she'd seen the bunnies do in the field. The fluttery things ringing the bowl of beer stopped fluttering, and their glow dimmed. Even the little thing on the back of the toad quit moving its tiny wings.

"I won't hurt you," Cecily whispered. "I brought you the beer. I wouldn't do that if I wanted to hurt you."

She was never quite sure what happened next. One moment she

was sitting in the lawn chair watching something that couldn't be real, and the next her aunt was bending over her.

"Cici, honey?" her aunt said. "What in the world are you doing sleeping out here on the grass?"

And she *was* on the grass. She still had the throw wrapped around her, but the lawn chair was empty beside her. The grass was damp and kind of scratchy beneath her, and the ground was hard. Overhead, the sky was pale blue and lavender and rose, and cloudless. The sun was almost up.

What had happened? Hadn't she fallen asleep in the chair?

Cecily sat up. "I think I had a dream," she said. "But I was in the chair."

Aunt Gin held out her hand. Cecily took it and got to her feet. She was stiff and cold, and she really had to go to the bathroom.

"What did you dream about?" her aunt asked.

"Bunnies." Cecily rubbed at her face with one cold hand. "And some little things that flew around and looked like fireflies, but not as big." She blinked as she remembered more of her dream. "And a toad! A big one, with a glowing butterfly on its back."

Aunt Gin's eyes widened a little, then she smiled. "So that's why my bowl is in the middle of the yard. You brought something out with you last night."

Cecily didn't want to lie to her aunt. Lying was wrong, her mom said, but more than that, it felt wrong to even think about lying to Aunt Gin. "Beer," Cecily said. "I brought them beer. You said bunnies and toads like beer, and I really wanted to pet a bunny."

Her aunt's face took on a strange expression. When Cecily thought about that morning now, she thought her aunt had looked wistful, but all ten-year-old Cici had cared about was that her aunt didn't get angry about the beer.

"That's fine," Aunt Gin had said. "But let's not do that again, shall we? I'll never hear the end of it if your mother finds out I let you stay outside all night long."

Cecily's mom didn't even like Cecily to go on sleepovers at a friend's house. Going to Aunt Gin's during the summer was the only sleepover Cecily ever had, and she didn't want to mess that up by disobeying her aunt over something Mom would ground her for.

"Okay," she said. "But I really want to touch a bunny. Do you think one will ever come in the yard for real and let me touch it?"

Aunt Gin put her arm around Cecily's shoulders and ushered her back into the house. "You never know," she said. "Around here, there's always a chance of bunnies, and occasionally even a toad."

Cecily didn't see any more bunnies in her aunt's backyard that summer. She did find the hole beneath the shrub that the toad had called home, although by the time Cecily found it beneath a bunch of dried leaves, all that was left was an empty hole in the dirt. The toad had moved on.

Three years later, so had Cecily's mom. Her job transferred her to a city far away, too far for her to send Cecily on a big Greyhound bus to Aunt Gin's for the summer.

Cecily had been thirteen then. She'd been disappointed, but there'd been Jason, a red-headed boy from school who played softball in the park during the summer. Instead of hanging around Aunt Gin's backyard, dreaming of touching a bunny, Cecily had hung out that summer with new friends at the park and watched Jason hit line drives over a low fence and flirt with other girls. Cecily forgot about bunnies and toads and her aunt, caught up as she was in the angst of her first unrequited teenage crush. Mom had said she was impossible to live with; looking back, Cecily tended to agree with her.

Years turned into a decade and then two, and Cecily never saw Aunt Gin again. Sure, she talked to her aunt on the phone whenever her mom said they could afford the call, and wrote her aunt letters when her mom said they couldn't. Aunt Gin sent Cecily a hundred dollar bill, the first hundred dollar bill Cecily had ever seen, when

Cecily graduated high school. When she graduated college, Aunt Gin had sent Cecily two hundred dollars in twenties hidden in the pages of Aunt Gin's latest fantasy novel.

A novel about talking animals who lived in the same world as people, even though most people couldn't see them.

The book reminded Cecily of the bunny and toad she'd dreamed about. Aunt Gin must have told Cecily the stories that formed the basis for her novels. That's why she'd had the dream about bunnies and toads and tiny lights that ringed a bowl full of beer.

After college came law school, and after law school the horrible years when Cecily worked eighteen hours a day, seven days a week, trying to distinguish herself from the other young associates. Her mom was proud of her—she told Cecily that often enough, after all—not that Cecily was surprised. Her mom valued hard work. Now that she was grown up and living on her own, Cecily understood what her mom must have gone through after Cecily's dad left home when she was only two. Cecily had no memories of her father, but her life had never really felt incomplete without him. She'd grown up with two women, her mom and Aunt Gin, who were strong, independent women in their own ways. It was no wonder that Cecily was so driven to succeed.

But at what cost? Standing in her aunt's empty house, she felt like she'd lost a lot leaving Cici behind.

She hadn't brought any beer with her to Aunt Gin's house. She'd never acquired the taste. Even if she had, she would have been afraid to bring any here.

What if she had, and the magic wasn't real?

Or even worse, what if it was?

The real estate agent probably thought she was nuts. She hadn't cared about any of the furniture inside her aunt's house. She'd told the man to box up all her aunt's books and personal things—Cecily would look over them later, when the loss didn't seem so immediate—but the only furniture she told the man not to touch were the lawn chairs she knew her aunt would still have in her backyard.

The maple tree was bigger than Cecily remembered. Of course, it would be. Unlike the house, it had continued to grow in the twenty years since she'd been here. The lawn chairs were newer versions of the ones she'd sat in with Aunt Gin beneath the branches of the trees, both of them swatting lazily at flies. The lawn was neatly trimmed now, as were the bushes and the flowers. The real estate people had hired someone to come in and spruce up the landscaping. Houses, especially forty-year-old homes, were a hard sell in the current market. She'd authorized the expense as both executrix and primary beneficiary of her aunt's estate.

An estate, she was surprised to discover, that included not only the house and the lot on which it sat, but the three lots next door that made up the empty field.

Over the years, her aunt had purchased the land. To keep it undeveloped and wild? It was too late now for Cecily to ask.

That was the other purpose for coming here. She couldn't decide what to do with all the extra land. With houses going unsold, no one was clamoring for empty land to build on. Cecily had a job and obligations a thousand miles away. Cecily owned all of the property, or would as soon as the estate closed, but Aunt Gin's had been her summer vacation spot, not a place she intended to call home.

Cecily brushed off one of the lawn chairs and sat down. The sounds of suburbia surrounded her. A neighbor a block or so away was mowing his lawn. Down the street, a dog barked, a playful yip. Somewhere else, children were laughing. Birds flitted from tree to tree, chattering at each other. A sparrow hopped along the top rail of the wooden fence between her aunt's backyard—now Cecily's backyard—and the field next door.

She unfolded the fan her aunt had used all those years ago. The spokes were thin wood, the brightly patterned fabric red silk. Aunt Gin had sent it to Cecily as part of her Christmas present just last year. Cecily had sent her aunt a gift card for a local restaurant as a last minute present.

"When did we lose touch?" she asked the empty yard. "Why did I let you slip away?"

The slats in the lawn chair creaked beneath her weight. In the field, some insect started a persistent buzzing.

That long-ago morning after she'd fallen asleep in this yard, before Aunt Gin had walked her into the house, Cecily had caught a glimpse of the bowl she'd brought into the backyard. She'd walked carefully out of the kitchen with that bowl, careful not to spill a single drop. It had been tricky because she'd filled it with beer almost to the very top.

The bowl, still sitting in the grass, had been empty that morning.

Cecily wondered if her aunt thought Cecily had finished off the beer, and that's why she'd been asleep on the lawn. The dedication in the fantasy novel Aunt Gin had given her for a college graduation present had been "For Cici, and the empty bowl."

Cecily's cheeks had reddened when she'd read that. She'd hoped her mom would never ask her what that meant. Only when her mom had called Cecily to tell her that Aunt Gin had died in her sleep in this very backyard had her mom admitted that she never read any of Aunt Gin's books.

Cecily shouldn't have been surprised. Her mom was much too grounded in the real world to believe in fantasy.

"Did I just dream that night?" Cecily asked the empty backyard. She must have. Things like beer-drinking bunnies and toads didn't exist. Not in this life.

The sun lowered in the western sky as Cecily sat in the lawn chair and thought about all the time she'd spent here. Aunt Gin's will had specified no funeral, no memorial. Cecily's mom had thought that was prudent. Cecily thought remembering her aunt in the place where she'd been the happiest was the best memorial of all, and she intended to take her time. She'd be going back to the real world of clients and deadlines and impossible hours soon enough.

The quiet yard and the warm day and the long hours on the plane caught up with her. She felt herself nodding off and thought for a moment that she should go inside and curl up on the little bed Aunt Gin had always kept for her in the small bedroom. Right about the time she remembered her aunt's furniture was gone, she heard a rustling in the grass.

She opened her eyes to see a rabbit sitting stock still on the lawn not three feet in front of her chair.

Cecily's breath caught in her throat. It couldn't be the same rabbit—bunnies didn't live that long—but it looked the same as the one she'd seen that early, early morning all those years ago. Soft brown coat, fluffy white tail, and dark, luminous eyes. Its ears were long and graceful. The only thing moving on the rabbit was its nose, tiny little twitches as it sniffed the air.

As it sniffed her.

Another movement caught her eye. There, at the edge of the field, was another rabbit. And another. And at the base of the fence, a brown toad, almost invisible against the dirt.

Had they all come to pay their respects to her aunt, like Cecily was doing?

But that meant they must have known that Aunt Gin was gone.

If she sat here long enough, would she see little pinpricks of light flutter out of the bushes in the back of the yard to light on the heads of the rabbits and the toad?

I'm too old for this, she told herself.

Or maybe she wasn't old enough. Aunt Gin had been in her forties when she moved into this house. Cecily had been a late-in-life child for her mother, and Aunt Gin was the older of the two sisters. Cecily had been surprised to learn that Aunt Gin was nearly eighty when she died.

Cecily made herself sit still. Soon the rabbits in the field joined the bunny in the yard. They all sat just out of her reach but close enough she could see their little noses twitch, all four of them.

The toad stayed by the fence.

"I loved her, too," Cecily said, her voice little more than a whisper.

She thought the rabbits might flee. Instead, one of them, the first one that had come into the yard, hopped slowly toward her. Nose twitching, ears cocked forward, it came toward her until it sat next to the right side of the lawn chair.

The one thing she had always wanted to do was touch one of the bunnies. Her mom would have been horrified. She would have reminded Cecily that rabbits carried rabies.

Her mom wasn't here. This had been Aunt Gin's home, a place where the magic was real no matter how old you were.

Cecily let her right arm drift slowly downward. She kept expecting the rabbit to run, but it sat there, watching her with its big, brown eyes.

She didn't try to touch it. She simply let her arm hang loosely at her side, her hand dangling in the air a few inches from where the bunny sat. The next move was up to it.

Starting with the rabbit next to her chair, they all touched Cecily's hand, one by one.

The first rabbit merely sniffed at it. Its nose was like a cat's, soft and rough all at once. She felt its breath on her skin, then it was gone.

The next rubbed its head against her fingers.

The third bunny butted her hand with its head, and as it passed by, her fingers trailed over the tips of its ears.

The last bunny sat next to her hand. Waiting.

Cecily moved her fingers until she could touch the fur on its back. The fur was incredibly soft and thick, like that throw from long ago. She could feel the rabbit vibrating, the nervous tension in its body making it seem almost like a purring cat.

Just about the time she wondered why it was so close to her if it was so nervous, the bunny sped away.

All four of them did, their fluffy white tails the only marker of their flight back into the field.

She hadn't seen the little lights again, but maybe she didn't need to. What had just happened with the rabbits was about as close to magic as a grownup was about to get.

Unless the grownup had been her Aunt Gin.

"What do you mean, you took the house off the market?"

Cecily's mom's voice was strident even over a cell phone a thousand miles away.

"What are you going to do with that place? It's not like the market's going to get any better."

Cecily didn't know how to explain it to her mom. She couldn't explain it to herself. She had no idea what she intended to do with Aunt Gin's property. Maybe she'd keep it for a vacation home, or maybe she'd chuck the whole ladder-climbing, junior-associate-trying-to-be-partner career path and move here. Aunt Gin had left Cecily more than the house. Cecily now owned Aunt Gin's literary estate, and Aunt Gin's books had done well. Cecily could live comfortably here while she studied for the bar in this state. When she passed the bar exam, she could figure out where to go from there.

She had time. She was only thirty-three. Aunt Gin had been in her forties when she'd bought this house, a little older when she bought the fields next door.

Cecily thought about her aunt's wide smile. The twinkle in her eyes. Her sense of fun. Had the magic in this place brought those qualities out in her aunt, or had her aunt's qualities attracted the magic that still lived here?

Either way, Cecily hoped that some of that magic, that good humor and enjoyment of life, would rub off on her.

Maybe, just maybe, she might even start calling herself Cici.

She thought her aunt would approve.

FIRST STEPS

The first steps were the hardest.

Jed used to tell her that back when they were both in junior high and she complained to him about having to walk the balance beam in gym class. Callie didn't have the world's greatest balance on land, much less on a four-inch wide beam of wood three feet off the ground.

"I'm going to break my neck," she'd said over a tray full of cafeteria food. "You just wait and see."

Jed had smiled at her. "Not your neck. Your arm, maybe, or your ankle. You know... stuff you don't need."

He'd stuffed a piece of french bread pizza into his mouth, pleased with himself. Callie would have smacked him a good one if Mr. Thedes hadn't been on lunchroom duty. Mr. Thedes had no sense of humor. He was almost as bad as Callie's dad, who *would* break her neck if she got herself suspended for fighting with her best friend in the cafeteria.

The first steps are the hardest.

Jed had been right, but he'd also been wrong. Second steps

weren't any easier. Sometimes all you could do was take one step after the next and let your body walk on automatic while your mind drifted away somewhere else. Someplace pleasant.

Wherever you needed to go to get yourself through what lay ahead.

Callie parked in an empty space in the back row of the nursing home's lot. Monday evening, only an hour left for visiting, no wonder the lot was only half full. Callie could have parked her car closer, but she needed the time—the extra steps—to prepare herself, especially tonight.

Would Jed know she was even there? Sometimes he did. Other times he thought she was his mother. Then there were the times he thought she was a total stranger, and she'd have to remind him that they'd been in love for decades, which broke her heart all over again.

But those times weren't the worst.

No, it was far worse when he thought there was nothing wrong with him and he accused her of punishing him by locking him away from the world. Jed didn't remember nearly setting the house on fire when he tried to cook bacon for himself in the middle of the night and left a pan of smoking hot grease on the stove. Or the time he left the front door wide open all day while Callie was at work, and their cat had gone outside to explore and never came back. He didn't understand that taking care of him had become more than Callie could handle on her own.

Jed was only sixty-seven years old, but he might as well have been a hundred. The disease that put him in a wheelchair was slowly eating away his mind, and there was nothing the doctors could do for him but make him comfortable.

No one could do anything at all for Callie. She was a sixty-seven year old widow whose husband was still alive.

Even their son said she should divorce him, but why? The expense of nursing-home care had already cost them their home. Now Callie lived alone in a small apartment that seemed empty and foreign and not at all like a home. She had no savings left, to speak of. She still worked, only part time now, for the same accountant she'd worked for more than thirty years, but her job would be gone soon, too.

Her boss had told her only that morning that he planned to retire at the end of the year. He'd already made arrangements to pass along his clients to another firm, one that wouldn't need Callie's help. She wasn't sure what she would do then. Social Security wouldn't provide enough for her to live on, and in a world where college graduates couldn't find a job, no one would want to hire a sixty-seven-year-old secretary.

Callie's worries about her own future had been one of the reasons she'd put off visiting Jed tonight. She was feeling too sorry for herself, too irrationally angry at him for putting her in this position—as if he'd had a choice—to be able to put on a happy face and take whatever his mental state was this evening with a calm, steady smile.

First steps, Callie girl.

She took a deep breath and got out of the car.

The late June evening was pleasant, the sun just a warm glow behind the mountain peaks to the west. The first stars were already well-established in the eastern sky. Forest Hills Nursing Center, an odd name for a nursing home in a desert state like Nevada, nestled against the foothills east of Sparks, far enough away from the neon and bright lights of downtown Reno that Callie had no problem seeing the stars. The location, plus the fact that she could get Jed a room with a window that let him see the eastern sky, was one of the reasons she'd chosen Forest Hills. When they were first married, they used to sit outside on summer nights and look at the stars.

Did he ever look at the night sky now? She didn't know. In the summer, visiting hours were over before it came on full night, and in the winter the staff closed the blinds in the patients' rooms when the sun went down to conserve on the heat.

Callie smoothed her sweater with her palms, took another deep breath, and strode toward the after-hours entrance.

The front entrance to the nursing home was locked at six every night, and late visitors, like Callie was tonight, had to use the side entrance. Nestled between two wings of the home, the side entrance had a push-button coded lock with a ridiculously easy-to-remember number sequence. As the staff explained, the lock was to more to keep wandering residents inside than visitors out.

Callie keyed herself in and made sure the door shut tight behind her. Inside, the hall was brightly lit with energy-saving bulbs. The floor was covered with off-white industrial-strength linoleum liberally speckled with black and gray flecks. Callie's low heels clicked on the floor as she walked past the physical therapy room and the darkened caseworkers' offices, all locked for the night. Straight ahead, the short hallway dead-ended at the main corridor. Jed's room was down the hallway to the right past a central hexagonal nursing station.

None of the nursing staff acknowledged her. She'd never seen them acknowledge any visitors. It was if they went about their business not wanting to know that their patients had families they'd left behind in the outside world. She wondered if that made taking care of the residents easier, somehow.

Jed didn't have a private room. Callie couldn't really complain. At least this roommate was sane. The last roommate had done nothing but moan every time Callie visited.

She'd asked Jed once if the man did that all day. Jed had replied that he didn't hear anything, and she must have been imagining things because he didn't have a roommate. Callie hadn't asked again.

The walls in Jed's room were painted a dull peach—a southwestern version of salmon—but in the blue-tinged light of the energy-saving bulbs, the color looked like sickly apricot. The light reflecting off the walls always made Jed's skin look sallow. Thank goodness the brightest of the lights had been turned off for the night. Only the low-wattage bulb of the head of Jed's bed was turned on when Callie got to his room.

Tonight the curtain separating Jed's bed from his roommate's was closed. Callie wondered if the wizened old man in the second bed had had a bad day. He was pleasant enough, always nodding at Callie whenever she visited and giving her a little finger wave with the arthritic fingers of his right hand when she left, but he never spoke to her. After the moaning roommate, she appreciated the man's attempt to allow her and Jed their privacy.

"Hello, sweetheart," she said as she walked into Jed's field of vision.

He was propped up in bed, pillows on each side of his head, his legs tucked beneath the thin, hospital-grade blanket. The head of the bed had been elevated so that Jed could lean back and still look like he was sitting up. The afghan Callie had crocheted for him covered the foot of the bed. His hands were resting on the top of the hospital blanket, his fingers worrying the thin cloth. He was looking out the window. He didn't turn his head toward her, and his eyes stayed focused on something outside.

"Jed?" she asked. "I'm sorry I'm late. It's been a busy day."

No response.

Callie sighed and sat down in the single visitor chair next to Jed's bed. It was going to be a long visit, even though she could only stay an hour until it would be time to leave.

She couldn't even watch television and pretend they were watching it together like they used to at night when Jed first got sick. The television mounted high on the wall in one corner on Jed's side of the room was turned off. Callie supposed she could have turned it on, but it didn't seem like she should. This wasn't really her room. It wasn't her chair or her television. She even avoided using the small bathroom when she visited here.

"I think I'm going to be out of a job soon," she said. "I'm not sure what I'm going to do with myself. Jasper says I can come live with him, but I told him no."

Their son, a civilian contract employee for the military, lived on the other side of the country in North Carolina. Jed might not always know she was here, but Callie couldn't bring herself to even consider abandoning him, much less think about moving him across country to someplace strange. She worried that the trip alone might kill him.

"You should hear him, Jed. You'd be so proud of him. He's doing fine, he says, and he doesn't want me to worry, he can take care of me. Can you imagine that? Doesn't seem all that long ago, I was walking him to school because he was nervous about his first day."

"First step's the hardest," Jed said.

Callie had been caught in the memory of that walk with her son to school, but now her attention snapped back to the here and now.

Had Jed actually responded to what she was saying?

She'd been staring at the blank wall, looking more at her memory than the ugly paint. When she turned her head to look at her husband, Jed was looking at her instead of gazing out the window. His eyes were clear blue with none of the rheumy, washed-out look so many of the patients here had.

That clear-blue gaze was disconcerting when he was off wandering somewhere in his mind, but now it was heartbreaking. He eyes looked exactly like they had the day they'd stood before the preacher in that wedding chapel downtown and said their vows on the stroke of midnight, just a couple of kids who had no idea what married life really meant.

She was almost afraid to break the silence and discover it wasn't really her he was looking at, only a stranger he didn't know. Finally she made herself say his name.

"Hi, Callie girl," he said in response. "It's a beautiful night outside. Too bad we can't go take a walk."

She blinked back a tight feeling in her chest that wanted to break out into a sob. Her Jed was back. She didn't know for how long, but she'd take what she could get.

He smiled at her. He always had a crooked smile, one side of his mouth tilting up higher than the other. It turned what her girlfriends back in school had called his plain face into something special. Callie had never thought his face was plain.

"I've been spending a lot of time looking out that window today," he said. "Never even put the television on. You want to watch something before you have to leave?"

Callie shook her head. Jed had been the one who always had to have the television on. Quiet houses weren't for him. "No, I'm good right like this."

"You bring anything to work on with you today?"

He meant her crocheting. She brought it sometimes on the weekends when she spent more time here. She liked to crochet by the natural light from the window. At night it was too dim in the room to see what she was doing.

"Not tonight, maybe when I come on Saturday. I started a new afghan for your bed, would you like that?"

His smile dimmed a little. "I won't be here on Saturday, honey."

Callie felt her own smile fade. She'd thought for a moment that things were just fine, that it was only his body that had betrayed him tonight.

Back when Jed's mind had first started to deteriorate, his doctor had told Callie that whenever Jed wandered away from reality—whenever he couldn't remember a name or a place or where he was—she should gently bring him back to reality without doing the remembering for him. She done that at the beginning, but ever since she'd realized he was never leaving the nursing home, she wasn't as diligent as she should have been. Tonight she was too disappointed in how briefly he'd been her Jed, and how swiftly he'd faded back into the stranger who lived in her husband's mind, to even try.

Instead of telling him that of course he'd still be right here on Saturday, she asked, "Where will you be?"

He looked out the window. "Flying around the stars."

"Like we used to talk about? Remember how we used to sit out on the deck and watch the stars?" They used to try to name the constellations but had given up. Neither one of them had the eye to pick out the shapes in the stars that the ancients had, so instead they'd talked about how wonderful it would be if someday people could actually fly to those stars for a visit.

"Something like that," he said. "Cicero's going to take me flying."

Cicero had been their cat, the one that had wandered out the front door and never came back.

Callie didn't know what to say, so she just sat back in her chair. Maybe it was a good thing there wasn't much time left on tonight's visit. This was all too much for one day. Maybe she shouldn't have come at all, not with the mood she was in.

"He could take you, too, if you want," Jed said. "It might be fun to go together." His gaze came back to her, and he leaned toward her as far as his body would let him. "I have to tell you, I'm a little afraid to take that first step by myself."

"First step's the hardest," she heard herself say, almost without thought.

"Yeah, that's what I always said, didn't I? Funny how giving advice is always easier than taking it."

This was always so hard. Talking to him like this, he sounded normal. He sounded like her Jed, but what he was saying just didn't make any sense.

"Sweetheart, do you even remember who Cicero was?" she asked. "Do you remember what happened to him?"

"I..." He leaned back against the bed, his little burst of energy spent almost like someone had cut his strings. "I think I did something, didn't I? I don't remember..."

"You left the door open and Cicero got out. You left the door open because you couldn't even remember such a simple thing like closing the door, and Cicero's gone. He's been gone for years. He's not coming back, he never came back, and it's all—"

Callie stopped herself.

A part of her was horrified at her rant—Jed couldn't help what happened to his mind—but another part of her, the part that missed her cat and her house and her life, was relieved that she'd finally said it. Cicero had been her baby, the cat who'd cuddled with her on the sofa at night and who wound around her ankles in the morning, begging for tuna. She'd been heartbroken when she'd realized what had happened to him, and she'd been furious with Jed. She'd just never let him know.

Until now.

"He's coming back." Jed's eyes were glistening. "This is me talking, Callie girl, and I'm telling you, he'll be here. You just have to have a little faith."

A little faith? "I'm worn out," she said. "I'm so tired. I'm afraid faith is a little beyond me right now."

"Then wait with me. If I can hang on long enough, I've got faith enough for both of us. I just need you here with me, to help me take that first step. Can you do that for me?"

Callie glanced at the big round clock on the wall. Ten minutes to nine. The nurses might not talk to any of the visitors who walked by the nursing station, but Callie was sure the staff wouldn't hesitate to kick her out if she didn't leave in the next ten minutes.

She sighed. She so wanted to believe that this was her Jed, and if it wasn't, she wanted him back before she had to say goodnight. It was easier to go to her little apartment all alone if she got to say goodnight to her Jed first.

"Okay, I'll wait."

The hands on the clock ticked off the minutes. They sat in silence in the dimly lit room, Jed looking out the window, Callie staring at the clock. When the minute hand reached the top of the hour, she got up from the chair.

"I have to go, sweetheart," she said.

"No!" He reached out with one hand and grabbed her wrist.

"You promised."

"They won't let me stay."

"Then hide."

The suggestion was ludicrous. Where could she hide? The room had a shared bathroom and a tiny closet where the staff kept extra adult diapers along with Jed's sweatpants and tee shirts and a jacket for the days they wheeled him to the central courtyard so he could get some fresh air.

"I have to go," Callie said as firmly as she could. His grip on her wrist was like iron. She'd probably have bruises she'd have to explain at work the next day.

"Please. I need you."

That did it.

Callie squeezed her eyes shut. Jed needed her. The stupid rules of this place, the rules that said a husband and wife who'd lived together for nearly fifty years couldn't spend one minute past nine o'clock at night in each other's company, didn't hold a candle to the fact that her husband needed her.

"All right," Callie said. "But where can I hide?"

"Under the bed. Remember when I did that at your house?"

Callie remembered.

They'd been best friends throughout junior high. It wasn't until their junior year in high school that friendship transformed into something more. The change had been so gradual that Callie hadn't been surprised at all the first time Jed kissed her. What had been surprising was her own reaction. She'd nearly lost herself kissing him back. By the time they surfaced for air, they'd both been half-undressed.

They spent almost every waking moment after that trying to get some time alone. Finally, frustrated beyond rationality, they'd concocted a plan where Jed would actually climb through the window in Callie's room late one night.

The plan would have worked if Jed hadn't thumped against the side of the house so loudly during the climb that the noise woke up Callie's dad. Jed had shimmied beneath Callie's bed and stayed there until her dad was satisfied the noise was simply the house settling. They still did what they planned to do, but they were quiet about it.

Her bed had been a whole different thing than the hospital bed. The hospital bed was higher off the floor and didn't have a handy dust ruffle to hide anyone crouching beneath the frame, not to mention all the rails and gears for adjusting the mattress.

At least she wasn't wearing a coat that would get caught on the frame, and she hadn't brought her bag of crocheting that would need to be hidden as well. She just had to stuff herself underneath the bed.

The linoleum floor was cold and hard on her knees. Callie got down slowly, all the while waiting for someone to come to the door of Jed's room and demand to know what in the world she thought she was doing, but no one came. She lay down flat on her back and skooched beneath Jed's bed.

After a few minutes, she remembered that she hadn't asked Jed how long she should stay here. Would she have to stay like this all night? She wasn't as spry as she used to be. If she stayed flat on her back on the floor all night, she might not be able to move in the morning.

Callie tensed when she heard rubber-soled shoes squeak on the linoleum as someone walked toward Jed's room.

"Your wife leave?" she heard a nurse ask. "I didn't see her walk out."

Jed didn't say anything, and the nurse grunted.

Callie breathed as quietly as she could when the nurse walked into the room, checked on Jed's roommate, and then lowered the head of Jed's bed and switched off the light. Callie watched the nurse's feet as the woman walked back to the door and closed it nearly all the way shut behind her.

The woman hadn't seen Callie beneath the bed, even though Callie knew she had to be visible. How in the world?

Callie slid out from beneath the bed and stood up slowly, holding onto the chair for support. When she finally managed to stand up straight, she saw Jed grinning at her even in the pale light from the street lights in the parking lot outside the window.

"That's my Callie girl," he said.

She leaned over and kissed him, smack on the lips. "That's the craziest thing I've done in years." And the hell of it was, it felt good. Even though her joints ached, she felt better than she had in years, too. "So how long do we wait?" She couldn't quite bring herself to say "for Cicero."

"Not long, now." Jed grabbed hold of her wrist again, but gentler this time.

Callie managed to slide the chair closer to the bed with her free hand without making too much noise. She sat down in the chair, and Jed went from holding her wrist to holding her hand. The chair was lower than the bed. She'd have no feeling in her hand soon, but it didn't matter. She'd stay until Jed fell asleep, or she'd fall asleep in the chair and someone would eventually find her in the morning. She'd deal with the fallout then.

She'd just closed her eyes and started to drift off to sleep when she noticed the light from the window getting brighter. That was strange. With visiting hours over, no cars should be driving through the parking lot, so no headlights should be shining through the window.

Callie opened her eyes, and her breath caught in her throat.

Cicero was outside Jed's window, sitting on the ledge.

He looked the same as he had on the day he'd wandered out the front door and never come home.

"Oh, Jed," Callie said, her voice soft. "You were right."

But how could that be?

The bed creaked, and Callie realized that Jed had let go of her hand. She sat up in the chair, rubbing at the pins and needles in her hand, and watched, incredulous, as Jed got out of bed.

Jed, who hadn't been able to walk for nearly a year, was standing on his own two feet. Without help. He couldn't even sit up in bed without help.

"Sweetheart, what's going on?" she asked.

He smiled at her. "I'm getting ready to take that first step. I'm glad you're here with me."

Understanding flowed into Callie like ice water, and this time she didn't try to blink the tight feeling in her chest away. "Oh, Jed. No."

She was still sleeping. She had to be. *Wake up*, she told herself. *Wake up and you can stop this. You can call someone for help, but you have to wake up!*

The glass in Jed's window dissolved as the light outside grew brighter. Cicero leapt from the windowsill onto the linoleum floor right in front of Callie. The cat turned his green eyes on her, blinked at her twice, and sat down, ears forward.

Callie reached down to pet him, half afraid her hand would pass right through the cat, but instead her fingers found his soft fur. She scritched Cicero behind one ear, and the cat started to purr before he jumped onto her lap.

The solid weight of him was so *real*, but he couldn't really be here. He couldn't. Just like the window couldn't really dissolve and Jed wasn't really standing on the floor, ready to take the first step.

His last step.

Cicero rubbed his head against Callie's chin. *There's always a guide.* Callie heard the words clearly in her mind. *No one ever goes alone.*

"Did you have a guide?" she asked the cat.

Yes. So will you, when your time comes.

This wasn't her time. She wasn't here to take that first-last step with Jed.

She was here to say goodbye.

Callie looked into her husband's brilliant blue eyes. "I love you, Jed Stacy. I always have."

He smiled that crooked smile at her. "Even when you wanted to slug me one back in junior high?"

"Even then."

Even now, when she'd been so irrationally angry at him for something he couldn't control, there'd always been love.

"I'll be waiting for you, Callie girl."

"I know you will."

"But you take your time. We've got all the time in the world to go flying to those stars."

"Promise?"

He didn't have to say it. She could see it in his eyes.

Cicero jumped down off her lap and walked over to Jed.

Time to go.

Callie wanted to stand up and kiss Jed goodbye, but all her strength seemed to have fled, and she knew her legs wouldn't hold her.

She sat in her chair and watched her husband take his first step. And his next.

She watched until Jed and Cicero faded from view, until the window reformed itself and the unnatural light faded from the sky.

When she finally stood up, she didn't look at the bed. Her Jed wasn't really there anymore. He'd never been hooked up to machines—he hadn't needed that level of care—and no insistent beeping or blaring interrupted the nighttime quiet to announce his passing.

Callie rubbed her wet cheeks and blew her nose in a tissue she took from the box at the bedside. There would be arrangements to make, and she would have to call their son. If he was serious about his offer to come live with him, she just might do that.

This time when she walked past the nurses' station, the night duty nurse looked up in surprise. "Mrs. Stacy? What are you still doing here? You know the rules."

Callie smiled at the woman. "It doesn't matter."

"It's a rule," the woman said. "We can't have visitors breaking the rules whenever they want."

"It won't happen again."

It was an easy promise to make. Callie wouldn't be back.

She let herself out the after-hours entrance, making sure the door shut behind her. The moon was rising over the mountains to the east. The night air was cooler now, and she was glad for her sweater.

As she passed by Jed's room for the last time on the way to her car, she looked at the window. Outside, with a slight breeze whispering against her skin and the city lights of Reno lighting up the night sky to the west, it was easy to wonder if she had really seen what she thought she had or if she was losing her mind, too.

She'd lived in Reno her whole life, and she'd never seen anything out of the ordinary. What had happened in that room was so far beyond ordinary, Callie knew she could never hope to explain it to another living soul.

Overhead, stars filled the night sky. Out of the corner of her eye, she thought she saw something streak across the sky.

Jed, taking his first steps among the stars with Cicero as his guide.

When her time came, she hoped Jed would be her guide. First steps were the hardest, but they were easier when you knew something—some*one*—was waiting for you on the other side.

ANOTHER DOOR

Mavis Trimble dug her husband's grave beneath the white oak tree where he'd proposed to her thirty-one years ago to the day.

It took her the better part of the morning to hack her way with a shovel through the first few inches of cold, root-choked ground. There were easier places to dig a grave, but Mavis hadn't picked the spot just because it was where Edgar proposed.

The white oak was the tallest tree in the windbreak behind their Iowa farmhouse, and Edgar had been a tall man. The rope swing Mavis's daddy had hung from the oak's branches was still there, frayed now with age. When she was a girl just beginning to notice that boys were good for something other than teasing, Mavis used to sit in that swing and dream about the handsome man she'd marry someday. Edgar hadn't been all that handsome, but he'd been a good, decent man who'd loved her with all his heart, and she'd loved him with all of hers. Mavis wanted to lay his memory to rest in a spot that was special to her no matter how much hard work it took to dig the grave.

Before the sun climbed high overhead, Mavis gave up on the

shovel and started attacking the rocks and roots with a pickaxe. She worked up a serious sweat as she got into a steady rhythm with her swing.

It felt comforting to be warm. The sun wasn't much good for that these days. The sky as far as she could see was filled with the same dark, ashy clouds that had been there the day before, and the day before that. The clouds made the sun look like a pale, pitiful ghost of itself.

She should have started with the pickaxe, but the pickaxe had been in the heavy equipment barn, and that had been Edgar's place. Mavis didn't like to go in the barn anymore. The tractor and cultivator and corn harvester they'd put themselves in debt to buy were her husband's babies, and they looked forlorn and abandoned without Edgar to take of them. No one had used the machines since her husband left to fight in the war. Mavis doubted anyone would ever need to use them again.

The life Mavis and Edgar had worked so hard to build for themselves was gone. The farmland might have been in Mavis's family for generations, but Edgar made it bloom. He'd planted hundreds of acres of corn year after year, an ocean of green that stood eight feet, ten feet high, almost as far as the eye could see. All that hard work had finally started to pay off. This year had looked like the second in a row their family farm would turn a profit.

Their ocean of green was dead now. The middle of August, and the stalks were brittle and dry and frozen, and like everything else in the world, covered with dry, dusty ash.

Mavis knew she should have worn a mask over her mouth while she dug, but did it even matter anymore? A coughing fit nearly doubled her over, and she had to lean on the handle of the pickaxe to keep herself upright.

"Pitiful," she said when she got her breath back. The grave she worked so hard to dig was twelve inches deep, if that. It was almost like the land was refusing to believe what Mavis knew in her heart.

"He's not coming back, you hear?" she told the farm. "I've accepted it. Why can't you?"

The only response was the slow, steady *vhump, vhump, vhump* from the wind turbine behind the silo.

At least the grave was finally long enough.

Mavis laid out her husband's best suit—hell, his only suit—on the dirt at the bottom. Deep, rich blue, the suit looked almost black in the sullen daylight. On top of the suit, she put her favorite picture from their honeymoon, a simple shot of the two of them smiling at each other over dinner. There hadn't been a lot of money, even back then. They'd stayed at the best hotel they could afford in Des Moines and promised each other they'd be back to celebrate their golden anniversary.

"Looks like neither one of us is gonna make that date, honey," Mavis said. "Not like we didn't try, but I guess the good Lord had other plans."

She added a few other trinkets to the grave. The ticket stub from the first movie Edgar'd taken her to. The Christmas card he'd given her the year they got married. His favorite baseball cap.

The last thing she put in the grave was the hardest. A baby blanket, the first of many she'd knitted back when they thought they'd have kids. After she'd turned forty-five, she'd given away all the blankets she'd made except for this one. Pink and blue and pale yellow, the blanket stayed at the back of the linen closet. Mavis always told herself it should go to someone special.

No one special was left in this world, not even her husband. She had no body to bury, no ashes in an urn to put on the mantle. Edgar was gone. This poor grave filled with clothes and memories and dreams was all she could do for him.

The breeze picked up. The photograph fluttered, and Mavis knelt to put a rock on it to hold it in place. She caught sight of the plain gold band on her ring finger. Did widows bury their wedding rings with their husbands? Mavis couldn't remember. It was the only piece of jewelry she owned. She smoothed the baby blanket with her left hand, and decided enough was enough.

Her knees creaked when she stood back up. "Pitiful," she said again.

The fields of dead corn rustled in the breeze, seeming to echo the word back at her.

Mavis grabbed the shovel and went about the task of filling up the grave. She pretended not to notice when the dirt covered the last bit of the blanket, then the last of Edgar's suit. She didn't stop working until she was coughing so hard she expected to see blood on the hand she used to wipe her mouth.

No blood. She wasn't dying.

Not yet.

The day grew so dark she could barely see the cross her daddy had built on the little rise a quarter mile away. He hadn't been an overly religious man, but her daddy had believed in God in his own way. He'd built that cross big enough to make sure it could be seen from every corner of their property. To remind them, he'd said, that God has a plan, even if man can't see it.

"I don't suppose you want to let me in on this one?" Mavis said to the cross. "Because I gotta tell you, I don't see a door anywhere around here."

That last little bit had come from Edgar. *When one door closes, another one opens,* he used to say. Same thing as saying God has a plan, although Edgar would never put it that way. He hadn't believed in God. What he believed in was the power of a positive attitude, and it had been one of the reasons Mavis had fallen in love with him. Without him, Mavis felt like all the positive had gone out of her life.

The cross didn't answer her any more than the land had. Mavis was alone, and she'd be alone until the day she died.

She looked down at the grave. "I'm trying, honey," she said. "I just don't know why."

She had one more thing left to do. She'd made a simple cross out of the slats from the back of one of the kitchen chairs. She shoved the cross in the ground at the head of the grave.

The marker for Edgar's grave bore his name on the crossbar, written with a permanent marker, along with the date of his birth. Mavis had almost left the date of his death blank, but in the end she'd written the date the world had died.

The date human beings learned they weren't alone.

The first movie Edgar had taken her to see all those years ago was *Alien*. He'd told her later he thought she'd be scared enough she'd want to hide her face in his shoulder, and it would give him an excuse to put his arm around her. He never knew how close she'd come to telling him right then and there that she never wanted to see him again, but in the end, she'd decided she liked his arm around her just fine.

Back in those days, neither of them had any idea aliens were real. Not aliens like the acid-dripping monsters in the movie. Those make-believe bugaboos were teddy bears compared to the creatures who used Earth as a battleground in a war that had not one blessed thing to do with humanity.

Mavis and Edgar had watched, stunned, as televised reports showed the first massive ships appearing over seemingly random spots around the globe. As it turned out, the spots weren't all that random. The first aliens wanted water and minerals, and they didn't bother to ask before taking what they came for. Mavis supposed they were no worse than people who plowed under anthills without asking the ants if it was okay, but it sure set a person back some to realize that in the grand scheme of things, people weren't all that high up the food chain. At least people didn't seem to be food, so from Edgar's way of thinking, it could have been worse.

Worse showed up right about the time the governments of the world were beginning to mobilize against the wholesale plunder of the planet. The second species of aliens were more aggressive than the first, and it became clear soon enough that they were here to kill as many of the other aliens as they could. Even though humanity wasn't the target, whole cities rapidly became collateral damage.

Edgar was Army Reserve, but he would have left to join the fight even if he hadn't been called to duty. Mavis heard from him once after he left. Right before the communications satellites were shot out of the sky, he called to tell her to stay put. None of the battles were heading her way, and he wanted her to be safe. Then he told her his unit had been ordered to defend Chicago.

That had been four months ago.

At first, Mavis did what Edgar told her to. She holed up at the farm, kept the lights off at night, and watched the skies during the day, fearing that one of those massive ships would settle over their farm and carve up the land.

Weeks passed, and no massive ships appeared. From time to time jets and odd-shaped fighters screamed overhead, but they always seemed to be headed someplace else as fast as they could go. One day Mavis thought she heard the faint sound of explosions carried on the wind. The next morning smoke shrouded the cornfields. More and more smoke filled the skies, until finally clouds and smoke became a constant grey ceiling, and fine ash started falling like misty rain. It didn't take long before the land got cold and the corn started to die.

Mavis was a sturdy woman used to doing for herself. After a month of watching the skies and living like a scared little prairie dog, Mavis told herself she wasn't going to live the rest of her life like that. Her nearest neighbor was over four miles away, another neighbor lived on a farm two miles beyond that. She started trekking to her neighbors once a week in Edgar's battered pickup truck. They shared what news could be had, which was precious little once the Des Moines radio stations quit broadcasting.

The last time Mavis made the drive, she'd found her closest

neighbors' farmhouse deserted. Their truck was gone and so was all their food. A note with a scrawled *we're heading to Des Moines* had been left for her tacked to the front door. At the next farm, she found her neighbor dead on his porch, his head bashed in. Mavis couldn't find his wife or his truck. She sped back to her farmhouse, pushing Edgar's truck as fast as it would go, and loaded the shotgun Edgar kept in the bedroom closet.

She took the shotgun with her everywhere she went on her farm after that, but no one came for her. No more jets or alien craft flew across the skies. Even the birds seemed to have moved on.

Her neighbors had asked her once why she didn't leave. She'd thought about her daddy's cross and Edgar's grim smile when he'd kissed her goodbye, and told them the farm was the only place Edgar would know where to find her when the war was over. They'd smiled at her, but their smiles weren't the happy kind. Mavis didn't need them to tell her they thought she was a fool. When she was alone at night in the bed she'd shared with Edgar for thirty years, she suspected that he might never come back. She just hadn't been ready to admit it to herself, not back then.

The night after she buried what she could of her husband, Mavis sat up late at the kitchen table. She had a bottle of whiskey and a glass on the table in front of her, but she hadn't taken a drink. The wind was howling outside, and the turbine had shut itself down as it always did when the wind got too strong and it had generated all the power the farm needed. Mavis used to hate the noise the turbine made, but now it was like the heartbeat of a constant companion. The turbine kept the lights on and the dark at bay, and she missed it when it went quiet.

The shotgun on the table next to the whiskey bottle was a whole different kind of darkness.

She wasn't the kind to take her own life, but someone might stumble across her farm one day. Someone hungry enough or desperate enough who wouldn't hesitate to kill her. She had a good deal of food put away in the pantry. Could she kill to protect what she had here?

What if what came after her wasn't human? Just because she hadn't seen any fighters or heard any explosions in weeks didn't mean all the aliens were gone.

But if they were gone, if the fighting was really all done, then why hadn't Edgar come home?

She stared at her wedding ring and realized she was a liar. The grave had been a lie. She hadn't accepted that he was gone forever. That's why she couldn't bury her ring.

"Whenever you get back, I'll be here," she said. "You hear me? I'll be right here."

She put the whiskey bottle back in the cabinet and went to bed.

The sound of the Edgar's truck trying to start woke Mavis from a fitful sleep.

The wind had died down in the night. The clock on her nightstand read six-fifteen, but it was still pitch black outside.

Mavis fumbled for the flashlight she kept in her nightstand drawer. The keys to truck were right there in the drawer next to all the keys for the farm equipment.

Someone was trying to take Edgar's truck. Hotwire the thing and steal it away in the dark. It didn't have much gas in it anymore, but that truck was the only vehicle she had other than the tractor she'd never driven. She might intend to never leave the farm again, but she didn't want that choice taken away from her.

Mavis grabbed the shotgun and stepped into her shoes. She knew her way through her house in the dark. She turned the flashlight off and rushed to the back door as quickly as she could.

The truck was parked in a three-sided lean-to at the back of the house. Mavis used to tease Edgar that his farming equipment got a barn of its own, but his poor truck had to sit out in the elements.

Edgar always planned to finish the lean-to one day, turn it into a real garage, but he'd never gotten the chance.

The hinges on the back door squeaked and the door creaked when it opened. Mavis wouldn't be able to go outside undetected. Before she could think too much about what she was doing, she threw open the back door and ran outside, cocking the shotgun as she went.

She half expected to get hit on the head or shot from somebody hiding in the night. When that didn't happen, she ran toward the front of the lean-to just as the truck engine finally caught.

"Hold it right there!" She jammed the butt of the shotgun against her shoulder and leveled it at the driver's side window.

Whoever was in the truck turned the headlights on. The sudden light just about blinded Mavis. Startled, she jerked her finger on the trigger, and the shotgun went off, blowing a hole in the door frame of the truck over the driver's side door.

The noise from the blast nearly deafened her. She staggered when the gun kicked back against her shoulder, but she stayed on her feet.

"Okay, okay!" She could barely hear the man's voice, but she saw him scramble down out of the truck. "Don't shoot me, lady! I didn't know anyone lived here. Just don't shoot me."

"Come out here where I can see you." She gestured with the shotgun. "Out in front of the headlights."

He was shorter than she was and looked younger by a good twenty years. His features and hair were dark, maybe Hispanic, and he had on a tattered National Guard uniform.

"What's your name?" she asked.

"Freddie Perez," he said.

"That your uniform?"

"What's left of it." He held his hands halfway up in the air. He didn't have a gun as far as she could see.

"You armed?" she asked.

He shook his head.

"Why not?"

He gave her an incredulous look. "Lady, I'm lucky I got out of there with my life, okay?"

"Out of where?"

"Davenport."

Davenport was on the Illinois border, over a hundred miles to the east.

"It's not there anymore," Perez said. "We tried to protect it, tried to get people out." He shook his head. "Look, I'm sorry I tried to steal your truck, but I gotta get back to the kids. They get scared by themselves, especially in the dark."

Kids? "What kids? Your kids?"

"No, look, can I put my hands down? I'm not gonna hurt you, I swear."

Mavis thought about it. She was going to have to trust him sooner or later. Either that, or shoot him. If she got close enough to pat him down or try to tie him up, she'd be too close to use the shotgun.

"I'll shoot you if you try anything," she said.

"I believe you."

He put his hands down slowly, then wrapped his arms around himself. Mavis was shivering too, and it wasn't just from nerves. The early morning air felt as cold as the middle of October.

"These kids," Perez said. "I found 'em about twenty miles outside Davenport, huddled up inside this empty gas station. Five of 'em, and nobody to take care of them except me. We've been doing pretty good, keeping out of sight during the day when we were closer to the combat zone, but now I figure we're far enough away, I should find them something to ride in, you know?"

Mavis let the barrel of the shotgun drop just a little. "Are you telling me you and these kids walked all the way here from Davenport?"

"Yeah, seems stupid, don't it? But it's not like people just got sick and left their stuff behind. I've been checking places that look deserted, but if the people are gone, so are their rides."

Behind Perez, Edgar's truck sat idling, eating up precious gas. Mavis thought about what she was doing for about half a second, then decided to stop thinking before she talked herself out of it.

"Get in," she told him, gesturing at the truck with the shotgun. "Let's go get your kids."

She rode in the passenger seat with the shotgun resting across her knees and the heater on the truck turned up as high as it would go. Mavis slept in a set of Edgar's thermal underwear these days, but without a coat, she was still cold.

Perez drove carefully. Probably trying to avoid ruts that might make the shotgun go off if Mavis got jostled around too much. She didn't ask him any questions, letting him concentrate on where he was going. She knew her property even in the dark, even with the corn stalks dried out and dead, but she imagined one row looked much like the next to someone who hadn't grown up on the farm.

Perez finally stopped about a hundred feet or so from where Mavis's farm road intersected with the county two-lane. He got out of the truck and whistled low.

Five children slowly appeared from the field, creeping out from between the rows of corn. They were all horribly thin. The oldest couldn't have been more than twelve, the youngest three. They stood uncertainly in the road and stared at Mavis.

She opened her door and smiled down at them. "C'mon," she said. "Get in."

They eyed her shotgun and didn't move.

In for a penny, in for a pound. Another one of her daddy's sayings.

Mavis unloaded the shotgun and put it on the rack in the back window of the pickup. "Better?" she asked.

The children looked at Perez. It was pretty clear they weren't going to move unless he said it was okay.

"Where are we going?" he asked Mavis.

"Back to the farm. I've got hot water and extra beds and food, and it looks like you could use some of all three."

Perez frowned at her. "You'd share what you have with us after I tried to steal your truck?"

It's what her father would have done. It's what Edgar would have done. He'd gone to war to save people just like these kids.

"Yes," Mavis said.

After the kids had cleaned up and gone to bed, Mavis sat at her kitchen table and offered Perez a drink of whiskey. He declined.

"What's your plan with these kids?" she asked.

"Plan?" Perez looked out her kitchen window. The clouds were steel grey, dark and angry looking. The sun was up, but the day was still dark. "Get them to someplace safe. With someone who can take care of them."

Mavis nodded. "What about you?"

He shrugged. "My family was in Chicago. No reason to go back there."

Mavis felt her breath catch in her throat, and for a second she thought her heart might stop beating. "Chicago?"

He studied her face. "Yeah. Why? You got somebody there?"

"My husband. Army Reserve. His unit was headed there, four months ago."

Perez's eyes went flat, emotionless.

"We started calling the guys that got here first leeches, you know, because they were sucking things dry. Made it easier to think about them like they were something we could pop with our fingers. The leeches put three of those monster ships of theirs right over Lake Michigan. When the bugs got here and saw all that water, they wanted it for themselves. The leeches, they didn't like that. Their weapons..."

Perez's voice caught in his throat. He shook his head. His eyes weren't emotionless anymore. Mavis could see him struggling for the detachment he'd had only a moment ago.

"I've seen pictures," she said as gently as her own aching heart would allow.

"I'm sorry, lady, but that ain't nothing compared to in person. Both of them, they could take out entire city blocks with one beam. Their explosive weapons vaporized everything for miles." He cleared his throat. "Davenport might be gone, but Chicago's not even a memory."

Mavis looked down at her hands. She'd clenched her fists so tight her fingers were white. Her gold wedding band dug into her skin.

"I'm sorry, ma'am," Perez said. "If your husband was there, he's gone."

Mavis nodded. She couldn't bring herself to say anything.

Tiny footsteps padded into the kitchen. Mavis and Perez turned to find the youngest of the children, a little boy, standing near the refrigerator. "Can I have a drink of water?" he asked.

Mavis shook herself. She would mourn for Edgar later. "Yes, you may," she told the little boy.

She got a plastic cup from the cupboard and ran water from the sink, then handed the cup to the boy.

When he was done, Mavis asked if he needed help getting back to bed. He shook his head and wandered back down the hallway. Mavis watched him until he disappeared into the room where the rest of the children slept.

Perez was staring at her intently. "You got running water?" he asked.

"We have—" Mavis paused, then started over. "I have a well here. The turbine keeps the pump running, along with everything else."

"And you got food."

"Some." What would have been a lot for just her wouldn't be as much for another adult and five children, but it was better than nothing.

Perez got up and went over to the kitchen window. He looked out at the farm, stared at the equipment shed. At the silos.

"My unit was mostly made up of college guys," he said. "Some smart people. They didn't think this stuff was going to last forever, not like nuclear winter or anything. They kept saying 'we just gotta make it through the rough stuff,' like it wasn't going to last a lifetime, only a couple of years, or not even that long. The bugs and the leeches, they're all gone now. Some stuff ain't never coming back, but here?" He shrugged. "This is your place, so it's your say so, but I think we could last it out right here. Rig up something in your barn so we could grow enough stuff to keep us alive until the sun comes back and it's warm enough to start growing stuff outside again. I was an Ag major back in school. I think we could figure this out."

Mavis hadn't allowed herself to think of the future. She'd lived day to day for so long, just waiting for Edgar to come home so they could get back to the lives they'd always planned, she almost couldn't comprehend the kind of life Perez was talking about.

"You don't even know me," she said.

He turned his head to look at her. He was almost as gaunt as the children, but when he smiled, Mavis thought she could see a hint of the boyish charm that must have made him a hit with the girls at school.

"And you don't know me, ma'am. These kids, they didn't know me either, but I figure what's left of the world should stick together, you know? If we're gonna start over, we have to start someplace."

Start over.

"My husband used to say, when one door closes—"

"—another one opens," Perez finished. "Yeah, my mom said that, too. Drove me nuts, but I guess it sank in."

Mavis took the whiskey Perez had declined earlier out of the cupboard and poured two small shots into juice glasses. She gave one to Perez.

"No argument this time," she said.

He took the glass. She raised hers, and he followed suit.

"What are we toasting to?" he asked.

She looked out the window. It was still too dark to see the cross her father had planted so many years ago, but she knew it was there.

"To Edgar," she said. "And open doors."

NIGHT PASSAGE

The road stretched in front of Joleen, a dark ribbon in the darker night. Something glittered on the asphalt ahead of her, but she couldn't tell if her car's headlights reflected off pieces of quartz or broken glass. Either one was a possibility. Even this far out in the desert broken beer bottles littered the sides of the road, twentieth century man's way of marking his territory.

Casey sat in the passenger seat pretending total interest in the ghostly shapes flying by her window. Joleen could tell her daughter still was angry by the tense set of her shoulders and the way she kept her face turned away from her mother.

Joleen steered around the mess on the road as best she could on the narrow, two-lane highway. She hoped it wasn't glass. The tires on her car were old and worn, and she was afraid glass would go right through them. The bright lights of Las Vegas had faded to a dim glow on the horizon far behind her and Goldfield was at least forty miles to the north. She didn't want to have to stop out here in the middle of nowhere to fix a flat, especially not at night. Except for gas, she didn't want to stop at all until she got to Reno.

"Are you hungry?" Joleen asked just for something to say.

Casey didn't respond. No one could do the silent treatment better than an angry thirteen-year-old girl.

"Because if you are, we've got snacks and sodas in the back seat," Joleen said, trying again.

A sigh. Not much, but it was a chink in the armor, something Joleen could work with. It would be a long, long drive if Casey decided to stay angry the whole way.

Maybe a little music would help.

"Why don't you find something to listen to?" Joleen fumbled for the tape case without taking her eyes off the road. "We're can't pick up a station out here, and if you're not going to talk to me, then I need something to keep me company."

This time she got the rolled-eyes, oh Mom look, but her daughter took the tapes and rummaged through them.

"I know you didn't want to move," Joleen said.

"Look, Mom, I don't want to talk about it," Casey said, slamming the tape case shut. "Like my opinion would mean anything anyway," she added under her breath. Thirteen-year-olds always added something under their breath, that first sign of future rebellion.

Joleen took a deep breath. "So what do you want to talk about?"

Casey popped the tape in and turned back toward the window. "Nothing," she said. "I don't want to talk about anything, okay?"

So much for that plan.

Rock music blared from the speakers. Obviously one of Casey's tapes. Joleen didn't know the name of the band, but at least it might keep her awake. If she didn't go deaf first.

Thirty seconds later, Joleen reached for the volume control. She actually liked most rock music but that last guitar riff made her fillings vibrate. She glanced down at the tape deck to make sure she found the right knob.

"Mom, look out!"

Joleen jerked her eyes back to the road. She caught a glimpse of a large animal right in front of them. Heart in her throat, Joleen spun the wheel hard to the left and slammed on the brakes. Not good. She made it past the cow—she could see now that it was a cow—without hitting it, but the car started to skid, tires squealing. The rear end of the car slid around toward the front, threatening to send them into a spin. Joleen turned the wheel back to the right and took her foot off the brake, praying that the car would right itself.

That's when the tire blew.

Casey screamed again. The steering wheel jerked in Joleen's hands as the car pulled in the direction of the blowout and onto the wrong side of the highway. Joleen struggled as hard as she could to control it, muscles straining, but trying to turn the wheel was like yanking on a jar lid that didn't want to budge.

"Help me!" When Casey didn't move, Joleen yelled louder. *"Help me!"*

Casey jumped but she grabbed the wheel, her hands next to Joleen's, and pulled. With the two of them working at it they managed to turn the car back onto the right side of the road, the left front wheel thumping as what was left of the tire shredded under the rim.

"Aim for the side of the road," Joleen said, and together they steered the car off the asphalt. Once the tires hit the soft dirt of the shoulder, the car slowed down. Joleen feathered the brakes until the car shuddered to a stop.

Casey jerked her hands off the steering wheel like it was molten metal and sat back in her seat, her face white and pasty in the reflected light of the dashboard. Joleen let out a long, shuddering breath and rested her head on the steering wheel between her hands. She wasn't ready to let go of the wheel just yet. She was shaking badly, and she didn't want Casey to know just how frightened she'd been. So instead Joleen sat with her eyes closed and let the delayed stress reaction work its way through her.

After a few minutes, Joleen felt Casey's light touch on her shoulder. "Mom?" Casey asked, her voice small and tentative. "Are you okay, Mom?"

Joleen took a deep breath and raised her head to look at her daughter. She forced a smile. "Yeah, I'm okay. I've got a few more gray hairs than I did a minute ago, but I'm okay."

Casey didn't buy it for a minute, Joleen could tell. She took one hand off the steering wheel and brushed a strand of hair off Casey's face. "How about you?"

Casey flinched away. "I'm fine," she said in a tight, clipped voice, turning her face back toward the window as she reached up to rearrange her hair.

Joleen should have known better. Casey didn't like it when her mom tried to fix her hair. But Joleen had hoped Casey would make an exception, just this once, for her sake. Right now Joleen needed her daughter, the one who used to share chair with her so they could cuddle watching television, not this angry adolescent stranger.

"You're fine, I'm fine, I guess the only thing that isn't fine is the car," Joleen said, suddenly very angry herself. "I'm going to go look at the tire."

Joleen heard Casey's muttered "fine" as she shut the door behind herself.

"Fine!" Joleen said, venting a little of her own anger at the night.

Joleen took a flashlight from the trunk and walked around to the front of the car. The tire on the driver's side was a wreck. "Dammit," Joleen said. Not only was the tire shredded to ribbons, the rim was bent. They would have to spend the night in Goldfield, or Tonopah if she could make it that far on her car's small emergency spare, and then hope that when the service stations opened in the morning, someone would have a wheel that would fit. At least she'd remembered to check the spare before they left.

Of course, the jack and the spare were buried under all the stuff jammed in the trunk. Once Joleen realized they had to move back to Reno, she sold or gave away a lot of their things, which didn't make Casey any happier about the move. What was left was either packed in the car or placed in storage. Joleen stood with her hands on her hips, staring at the open trunk. It didn't look this full when they left.

Joleen walked around to the passenger side and knocked on Casey's window. After a minute Casey rolled it down. "I could use some help," Joleen said.

Casey got out without a word and trailed along behind Joleen to the back of the car.

Joleen nodded at the open trunk. "We need to unload all this so I can get the spare."

"You've got to be kidding me. Mom, it took us forever to get it all in there! And where are we going to put it?"

Casey's whining was the last thing she needed. Especially now. Not trusting herself to answer, Joleen hefted a suitcase out of the trunk and set it on the shoulder of the road behind the car.

Casey stared at her, her mouth open in disbelief. "You're just going to put all our stuff in the dirt?"

"If you have a better idea, go for it," Joleen said, grabbing a shopping bag full of shoes. "At this point I don't care, I just want to change the tire and get out of here."

Joleen dropped the bag next to the suitcase. She watched Casey out of the corner of her eye as she stood there. That was another thing about thirteen-year-olds. Most of the time they did what you asked, just not immediately.

Finally Casey slung a duffel bag over her shoulder, picked up a box, and walked around to the driver's side of the car. She put the bag on the floor next to the peddles and the box on the seat.

"Hey!" Joleen said. "That's my—"

"You're going to be changing the tire, not driving. Why can't I put it there?"

Joleen had to admit she had a point. "Good idea," she said.

Casey walked back to the trunk and lifted out another duffel bag. "You say that like you're surprised. I'm not a baby anymore, Mom. I can figure stuff out."

Joleen dropped a heavy box of dishes on the shoulder. "I never said you were a baby."

"That's the way you treat me." Casey's face was carefully neutral, but she was concentrating a little too hard on picking up a suitcase out of the trunk. Joleen recognized the look. For Casey, this was about more than just figuring out where to put things.

"If I did, I didn't mean to," Joleen said, choosing her words carefully. "I know you're not a baby anymore."

"Then why don't I get a say in where we live?"

"Casey..."

Casey looked up from the trunk, her eyes angry and accusing. "And why do we have to move, anyway? It's not fair. You get to make all the decisions but you won't tell me why."

They were back to that. This time it was Joleen's turn to look away. "It's complicated, Casey," she said, staring out at the desert. Joleen tried to pick out shapes beyond the reach of the narrow flashlight beam. She wondered if she should be worried about coyotes.

"See, that's just what I mean!" Casey said. "You act like what I think or what I want or what I feel doesn't matter. You treat me like a baby!" Joleen heard Casey sniffle and realized she was crying. "I'm not a baby, Mom. I'm not."

Joleen looked back at her daughter. It could have been a trick of the light, the open trunk light and flashlight casting strange shadows, or maybe it was because Joleen knew they could have both been killed if the car had rolled when the tire blew, but Casey looked different somehow. Older. Standing there wiping her nose with an angry swipe of her arm, tears spilling down her cheeks, Casey no longer reminded Joleen of the baby she'd held in her arms, the baby who used to keep her up all night wanting to play. That curious double exposure Joleen always saw whenever she looked at her, a blending of Casey then and Casey now, wasn't there anymore.

Joleen felt something inside break as she realized her baby girl was gone forever. She looked down at the ground. She needed to begin letting go. Life was going to be difficult for both of them in the next few months. Casey was going to need to grow up fast, and Joleen had to let her.

Now was as good a time as any to start.

"You're right," Joleen said when she trusted her voice again.

"What?" Casey asked around a sniffle.

Joleen handed Casey a tissue she'd stuffed in the pocket of her jeans, then lifted out the last suitcase and bag between her and the well where the spare tire and jack were hidden. "Don't look so surprised. I said you were right." She dropped the luggage behind her and lifted up the false bottom of the trunk. "Here, can you hold this for me?"

Casey held up the fiberboard panel covering the spare and looked at Joleen like she'd suddenly sprouted antenna or a bushy tail. Joleen spun the nut holding the spare loose. "I think I just had an epiphany, that's all," she said.

"Epiphany?" Casey echoed, wiping her nose again. "I never heard you use that word before, Mom. Are you sure you're okay?"

Joleen laughed a little. "Don't worry, your mom hasn't gone off the deep end. Wasn't that word on one of your vocabulary lists last year?" With a grunt, Joleen lifted the spare out of the trunk and leaned it against the back bumper. "Anyway, I remember it from somewhere and I think it fits." She stared down at the scissor jack. "I just hope I remember how this thing works," she muttered, picking up the pieces.

Joleen took the jack and lug wrench to the front of the car. She crouched down and aimed the flashlight beam underneath the car. She heard Casey drop the panel back in place, and the next thing she knew Casey had rolled the spare up next to her.

"What are you doing?" Casey asked.

"Looking for the frame," Joleen said. "You can't put a jack just anywhere, not on a car this old. If it's in the wrong place it'll bend the metal instead of lifting the car."

"Can I see?"

Joleen hesitated only a moment. "Sure," she said. Casey bent down next to her, twisting her body around until she could see where Joleen was pointing the light. "That's the frame," Joleen said.

"So the jack goes like this?" Casey asked, sliding it underneath the car.

"Yeah, just like that." Joleen held the jack in place and turned the handle until she felt it snug up against the frame. "Now this is the fun part."

"Fun?"

"Lug nuts." Joleen popped off the hubcap. Fitting the wrench on the first nut, Joleen jerked down hard on the crossbar. The nut didn't budge. "They put these things on with air guns," she said. "Sometimes this is a real pain." It took her three tries to break the nut loose.

One down, four to go.

"How come you're not taking them all the way off?" Casey asked.

"All I want to do is loosen them up a bit." Joleen went to work on the next nut. "If I wait until I jack up the car to do this, the tire would just spin and you'd have to hold it for me. And if I take them all the way off now, the tire might shift and bend the bolts. It's just easier this way."

Casey was quiet for a moment. "Did Dad teach you how to do this?" she finally asked.

"No, not your dad. He was never very good with cars."

"Then who did?"

Joleen smiled. It had been so long ago, she'd nearly forgotten. "When I first started to date, I went out with a guy named Mike." She broke the last nut free without a problem. "Mike loved two things in life and one of them was cars. I was just learning how to drive and Mike thought I needed to learn how to change a flat. Guess he was right."

Joleen put down the lug wrench and started cranking the jack handle, grunting with the effort as the jack slowly scissored up and lifted the wheel off the ground.

Casey grinned at her. "You said two things. You were the other one, right, Mom?"

"Me?" Joleen shook her head. "No, the other thing Mike loved was himself. We didn't date for very long."

Joleen stepped back, wiping her hands on her jeans and trying to judge whether the car was high enough to put on the spare. She thought it might be but she gave the jack handle an extra turn just in case.

"Sounds like he was a jerk," Casey said. "A useful jerk, but still a jerk."

"It was a long time ago. I'm just glad he taught me about cars."

"Yeah. Me, too."

Joleen spun the lug nuts all the way off and put them in the hubcap like Mike taught her, and then it hit her. That was the first time she'd talked to Casey about anyone she'd dated other than Casey's dad, and even those conversations had been vague, heavy on half-remembered good times, light on reality. The good old days hadn't been all that good and Joleen always thought Casey didn't need to know that. But talking to her about Mike just now had been so easy and natural, it made Joleen wonder. Maybe she'd been wrong about that. Maybe she'd been wrong about a lot of things.

"Mom?"

"What?" Joleen lifted the heavy wheel and what was left of the tire off the car. The rim was useless and she thought about leaving it off the side of the road but decided against it. She wasn't about to add any more trash to the landscape.

"What did you mean when you said you had an epiphany?"

She glanced at Casey. Her daughter was drawing designs in the dirt with the toe of her tennis shoe, staring intently down at her artwork.

Joleen almost said "nothing, really" but stopped herself. That was the answer she'd have given Casey yesterday. It wasn't the right answer now. "It's just that I realized something kind of important," she said finally. "Something that made me look at things a little differently."

Joleen rolled the spare in place and lifted it up, adjusting it until the bolts threaded through the holes. It was so small, it looked silly hanging there. When she first learned how to do this, spares were full size just like other tires, not like these emergency spares.

"Anyway, what I realized is that whenever I looked at you, a part of me still saw the way you looked when your dad and I brought you home from the hospital, how cute you were in your first Halloween costume, or how you cried your first day of school. And maybe, without even realizing it, I was still treating you like that little girl who refused to take naps in kindergarten and who thought Bobby McNeil was the coolest boy in first grade because he had a pet tarantula."

"Bobby McNeil was a dork," Casey said. "And his tarantula gave me the creeps."

"You say that now, but back then..." She glanced over at her daughter, checking to see if the tease was working. Casey stood there glaring at her, but at least it was a glare without venom.

"The point is, I realized you're growing up and all those memories should stay just that, memories." Joleen threaded the first lug nut back on its bolt, turning it until it made contact with the rim. "In a couple of years you're going to be learning how to drive one of these things, you're going to be making more and more decisions on your own, and as much as I need my little girl sometimes..." Joleen stopped, uncomfortably aware that all of sudden her voice was unsteady. She concentrated on replacing the rest of the lug nuts, trying to give herself time to get her emotions under control.

Casey stood and watched her, not saying anything for the longest time. "So why did we leave, mom?" she finally asked in a voice almost too soft for Joleen to hear.

Joleen stared at the tire without really seeing it. None of her old responses would work, not anymore. Casey was right, it was her life, too. She deserved to know why.

"I need to go home, Casey," she said. Such a simple answer, and so very complicated a response.

"But Las Vegas is home! That's where we've always lived."

"That's where you've always lived." Joleen turned the jack handle, letting the car down slowly. "I moved there when I married your dad because that's where he was going to school, but it never felt like home to me, especially not since he died."

Casey frowned at her. "That was a long time ago."

"Yes. Yes, it was," Joleen agreed.

"So why now? You waited this long, why now?"

Joleen pulled the jack out from under the car and realized her hands were shaking. She had hoped this conversation could have waited, waited until Casey was a little older, waited until she figured out how to tell her. Waited until she could figure out how to come to terms with it herself without falling apart.

She still couldn't quite bring herself to say it. Not out loud, not to her daughter. That would make it too real, and she couldn't handle that.

"We don't have anyone in Las Vegas, Casey," Joleen said slowly. "Any family or close friends. Anyone I can trust to take care of you."

"Why would you need anyone to..." And then Casey knew, Joleen could see it in her face. She was a smart girl, and she was right. She could figure things out.

"You lied to me, Mom," Casey said. "You're not okay, are you? Are you?"

Joleen couldn't stand to look at her daughter, at the pain and anger and betrayal she saw on Casey's face, but Joleen wouldn't let herself look away. "I am, for now. And I plan to be for a long time."

Casey glared at her. "What is it?" she asked, her tone daring her mother to lie to her again. "Or am I not old enough to know?"

It was real. Joleen had to say it, name it, face it. She couldn't hide from the truth by running away to her childhood home. The only home that really mattered was standing right in front of her.

"Cancer," Joleen said, barely getting the word out. "I have cancer."

Casey's anger dissolved. Joleen saw it melt off her face as shock took over. Casey stood there for a moment, looking scared and miserable, and then she threw herself into Joleen's arms. Joleen held her daughter while she cried, telling her not to worry, that everything would be okay. Gradually Joleen realized that Casey was telling her the same thing.

Joleen didn't know how long they stood there, but eventually Casey quieted and she pulled away. Her hair hung in her face, wet strands plastered to her cheeks. Joleen brushed it back before she could stop herself. "Sorry," she said, trying to smile. "I forgot."

"It's okay, Mom," Casey said, wiping her face and pushing her hair behind her ears. "Just don't make a habit of it, okay?"

"Deal."

Casey looked at her a moment longer then bent to pick up the hubcap. "So this goes back on now, right?" she asked.

"Almost." Joleen realized her own face was wet. She wiped it dry with the back of her hand. "First we have to make sure the lug nuts are really tight, then we can put the hubcap back on."

Casey put the hubcap down and picked up the wrench. "Show me how," she said.

ESSY AND THE CHRISTMAS KITTEN

The kitten looked like a cross between a drowned rat and one of those scary-looking bats with huge, radar ears.

Essy had been on her way out to scrape the latest accumulation of heavy, wet snow off her ten-year-old Toyota, a car that hadn't tried—yet—to kill her by deciding all on its own to set a new land speed record, when she saw the kitten huddling beneath the prickly holly bush at the corner of her house. Its ginger fur was sopping wet. Even without bending over to get a closer look, Essy could see it shivering as each new flake settled on its skinny body.

What in the world was a kitten doing out here all by itself? At the end of November?

Essy didn't exactly live at the edge of civilization, but her house was the last on the block. Beyond her fence, the land rose up into the first of the rugged foothills that separated her subdivision from the newest cookie-cutter shopping center in the valley a mile away. People didn't usually dump unwanted animals on her street. It was a dead end, which had suited Essy just fine when she bought her little house.

She supposed someone could have tossed the kitten out of a car and driven away. Or a coyote could have gotten its mother, even though a kitten seemed like easier pickings.

Essy had no pets. The days of pets and kids and a husband and work were long gone. But she couldn't leave a kitten out in the snow to freeze to death.

She crouched down in front of the bush, her knees protesting. The kitten backed a couple of steps away, crying at her, all wide blue eyes and pointy baby teeth. It couldn't have been more than eight weeks old, if that.

Essy's daughter had brought a baby kitten home one day from school. Six weeks old, and little more than a fuzzy black fur ball on spindly legs. "Mommy, can I keep her?" Essy and her husband had never been able to say no, not when their daughter had her heart set on something, so the kitten had joined their family. It was gone now, too.

"Come here, sweetheart," Essy said to the sopping wet kitten. "Where's your momma, baby?" She took off one leather glove and held her fingers out, hoping to entice it, but it backed away one more step, still crying.

Essy couldn't take hunching down like that for long. She already had too many aches and pains, and the cold only made them worse. She had to stand back up. At least the kitten didn't run away when she moved. "Are you hungry?" she asked it. Her daughter's kitten had always come running for food.

Tuna was a staple in Essy's kitchen. Easy food. Open a can, mix with mayo and dijon, eat in front of the television. Lather, rinse, repeat.

Back inside her warm house, in her tiny kitchen, Essy opened a fresh can. She mashed the hard flakes with the liquid in the can to make a kind of gruel and spooned a little on a saucer. She half expected the kitten to be gone when she got back outside, but it was still crouched beneath the holly.

"Here you go." She put the saucer down on the snow as close to the kitten as she could get, then backed away. Her car still needed scraping. She shuffled around the holly bush, giving the kitten a wide berth, and trudged out to her car. Only three inches of snow, but the local weather forecast said to expect another six inches by nightfall along with plummeting temperatures that would turn the slushy snow to ice.

Her neighbors on the downhill side of the street already had their Christmas lights out. LED icicles hung from the eaves of their garage, brilliant cold white light against the softer white of the falling snow. A group of wire-frame reindeer grazed in their yard, more clear bulbs illuminating their white bodies. The only color in her neighbors' yard were the plastic red and white candy canes lining their front walk.

Essy hadn't decorated for Christmas. She didn't intend to. Her Christmas decorations were packed away in the attic in plastic tubs, all neatly labeled with her daughter's blocky print. Essy couldn't stand to look at them.

Once the car was as snow-free as it would get considering the still-falling mush and Essy had shoveled away the accumulation of snow behind the tires, she approached the holly bush as quietly as she could. Even with her gloves, she couldn't feel the ends of her fingers, and her nose was starting to run. Either the kitten would let her come near or it wouldn't, but Essy couldn't stay outside much longer.

The saucer was empty, as clean as if she'd taken it out of the dishwasher.

The kitten was on her front porch, right in front of her door.

Essy huffed. "Now you have the sense to come in out of the cold," she said to the kitten. "You couldn't have figured that out sooner?" Kids, animal or human. Some things never changed. In a way, that was a comforting thought.

The question now was whether the kitten would let her pick it up.

Essy retrieved her saucer from beneath the holly bush and put it in the pocket of her coat. The kitten yelped. Before its cry had been the scared sound of a baby unable to cope with the world. Now its message was clear: more tuna.

"You're a hungry little baby," Essy said.

She approached the kitten slowly and again held her hand out, glove off, palm up. Instead of backing away, the kitten took a tentative step toward her and lowered its head toward her hand. When it finally touched the tip of her finger, Essy was shocked at how cold its poor nose was.

"That's right," she said, her voice as soft and soothing as she could make it. "You poor, freezing baby. There's lots more tuna inside. You just have to let me pick you up."

Essy didn't move as fast as she used to. If the kitten ran, she'd never be able to catch it.

When the kitten took one more step toward her, still sniffing her hand, Essy reached around the tiny body and lifted. The kitten yelped again and squirmed, but Essy had wrapped her fingers around and between its little legs. She brought the kitten in close and tucked it beneath her coat. The cold wet from its fur soaked through her shirt.

Essy's house was small, a foreclosure she'd bought outright with the insurance money and the little bit of profit she'd made selling the house she and her family had called home for twenty years. She had a bedroom, a guest room she'd turned into a library, a kitchen barely big enough for one, and a living room with a few pieces of furniture she couldn't part with. Her husband's recliner. Her daughter's desk. The sofa they'd bought the year their daughter graduated from high school, the first sofa they'd ever owned that wasn't second hand.

She could shut the doors to her bedroom and the library to keep the kitten out, but it was small enough it could hide under the sofa.

Essy didn't want to have to get down on her knees on her hardwood floor. Better to take the kitten into the bathroom, a small, contained space with no real place to hide.

Essy shut the bathroom door behind herself and took a hand towel out of the linen closet. The towel had belonged to her mother-in-law, years gone now too. Essy wrapped the towel around the kitten and began to rub gently. To her surprise, the kitten began to purr.

"Well, now," Essy said, looking into baby blue eyes. "Shall we see what you look like when you're not all wet?"

It took a little while, but gradually the kitten started to look like a kitten again. It was a ginger tabby with a sweet white face and white mittens on its two front paws. A very fuzzy ginger tabby. And hungry. It nipped at Essy's fingers as she continued to dry its fur.

Once she was done, she gave the kitten more tuna. While it ate off the saucer in the bathroom, Essy made a make-shift litter box out of an old aluminum cake pan and shredded newspapers that she kept for fireplace kindling. She put another towel down on the floor so the kitten wouldn't have to sleep on the cold tile, and left it alone in the bathroom to get used to its surroundings.

Essy had been watching an old Tom Cruise movie on cable before she first went out to scrape snow off her car. The movie was over. Now *It's a Wonderful Life* was playing. The first of the holiday movies.

Essy grabbed the remote and channel surfed. She clicked past shows on holiday meal planning, holiday shopping, Christmas episodes of decades old sitcoms. She turned the television off, and her house got quiet.

She used to watch all the holiday shows. She had storage binders full of Christmas DVDs and CDs gathering dust in the attic along with the tubs of holiday decorations. She had rewatched *White Christmas* so many times her family gave her a new copy every year in her Christmas stocking. She'd start playing Christmas music in her Toyota before Thanksgiving and kept it up after the new year until her daughter threatened to hide the CDs. Now she couldn't stand any of it. If there had been any justice in the world, Essy would have been able to skip directly from September to January. Do not pass go. Do not collect two hundred dollars.

Essy threw the remote down on the sofa. Her gaze passed over her husband's empty chair and paused at her daughter's dusty desk, the old computer chair with the broken arm snugged in tight against the scarred wood. Her daughter's computer was another empty, dark screen, just like the silent television; two vacant eyes that looked out over a lifeless room. Essy never turned her daughter's computer on, but she couldn't get rid of it either.

In the bathroom, the kitten cried.

Essy looked down at her lap. Her hands were warm again, but they were trembling.

"What can it hurt?" she said to no one. The worst that could happen, she'd bruise her knees getting the kitten out from beneath the couch.

No, that wasn't the worst that could happen. Not by half.

Essy got up, rescued the kitten from the cold, lonely bathroom, and sat back down on the couch. She deliberately turned her back on her husband's empty chair, on her daughter's dusty desk.

As the kitten snuggled against her neck, Essy opened the book she'd been reading that morning. Outside the late afternoon sky darkened and the snow continued to fall. Inside, Essy and the kitten both fell asleep.

The old pet store where Essy used to buy food for her daughter's cat was still in business. Back in the day, the place had been owned by a gentle-hearted woman who collected donations for animal rescue groups and conducted low-cost vaccination clinics twice a month. The woman always used to tempt Essy with playful kittens who needed a loving home, but Essy and her husband thought one cat in the house was enough.

When Essy walked in, stomping snow off her boots on the little rug inside the door, she was surprised to see the same woman standing behind the register. It had been years, but the woman remembered Essy, it was obvious by her expression. At least she had the good graces not to make a big deal of how long it had been since they'd seen each other. Instead she nodded at Essy, a small smile on her lips, and went back to waiting on the other lone customer in the store.

Essy passed over the familiar food she used to buy. That was for an adult cat. She selected a bag of kitten food, a kitten-sized food dish, and a real litter pan along with a small bag of litter. She turned around, ready to make her way to the register, when she saw a display of cat toys.

Her daughter's cat had actually fetched little plastic toys just like a dog. Throw the toy, the cat would go retrieve it, and drop it back at her daughter's feet, waiting for the next toss. It had been the silliest thing. The cat had also chased laser pointers, but her favorite toy had been a bit of loofa shaped like a mouse with feathers for a tail. The loofa hadn't been infused with catnip, but that didn't matter. The cat still made a one-cat game out of batting the thing all over the house.

The store had one of the loofa mice hanging in the display.

Essy hesitated. The kitten was still just a baby. That morning it had played with the shoestrings on Essy's tennis shoes, but its play was still tentative. The loofa mouse was too big for it. Besides, Essy intended to keep the kitten only long enough for the city road crews to clear the icy snow from streets between her house and the animal shelter. The kitten deserved a real home with a real family, not some empty shell of a house. Essy hadn't even given the kitten a name.

Then again, the toy only cost a couple of dollars. Essy had the money. What else was she going to spend it on?

She added the toy to the stack of supplies in her arms.

"Hey, there," the store owner said with a smile when Essy went to pay. "You have a new kitten?"

Essy recognized the small talk for what it was—an attempt to get over any awkwardness. The woman knew what had happened to Essy. It had been in the headlines for a week. Essy would take inane small talk any day over expressions of sympathy from someone who was practically a stranger.

"Just a stray," Essy said. "I'm not going to keep it."

"Oh."

Essy glanced away from the concern in the woman's eyes. She'd aged, just as Essy had. She had more grey in her long hair, more lines at the corners of her mouth.

"Hard time of the year for kitties," the woman said as she rung up Essy's purchases. "Too many people can't keep their homes, much less their pets. I'm fostering a couple of elderly cats now, but it's going to be tough to place them."

For a minute Essy thought the woman was going to try to talk her into taking another cat, and she experienced an odd sense of un-reality. The last few years couldn't really be what her life had turned into, could it? If she rushed out of here fast enough, would she get home and discover that the emptiness had only been a bad dream?

"I wish you the best of luck," Essy said. She grabbed the bag of kitten supplies and hurried out to her car.

Essy drove home as fast as the icy roads allowed, trying to hold onto that sense that everything would be just fine if only she could get home right now, but when she turned onto her street, she real-ized how foolish she'd been. This wasn't even the right house. A new family lived in her old home. They were busy making new holiday memories in the place where Essy had been the happiest in her life, and in the place where she'd experienced devastation so overwhelm-ing she still didn't know how she survived it.

"Stupid," Essy said.

Nothing had changed. She was still alone. She would always be alone. She only had a temporary boarder. Even if she kept the kitten, eventually it would die and leave her alone. Essy didn't think she could take the heartbreak. Not again.

Never again.

That night it started flurrying again. By the morning, nearly a foot of snow blanketed Essy's house and car and the roads. There'd be no taking the kitten to the shelter that day. Maybe not for days.

Not that the kitten seemed to mind. It had taken to bouncing around Essy's living room and kitchen, all spindly, fuzz ball legs and flagpole tail and ears that were still too big for its head. Whenever Essy sat down in her favorite spot, the kitten would scale the sofa like it was Mount Everest, sharp little kitty claws sunk deep in the fabric, until it reached Essy's shoulder. It liked to nestle in against her neck, its little cold nose against her skin, and purr. If Essy left it there, it would fall asleep.

"You're such a snuggler," Essy said, distracted from her book by the warm ball of purring kitten on her shoulder. "How could anyone dump a cutie like you?"

She rubbed behind one of the kitten's ears, and it purred louder. It reminded her of one of the toys her husband had brought home to her once, a round fur ball from an old science fiction show, a funny little thing that rewarded Essy with a mechanical chirp and purr when she picked it up. The one her husband bought must have been defective because it would chirp and purr at the oddest times, even when no one was touching it, but it never failed to make them laugh.

They'd never given each other traditional gifts. Toys and movies and music, those were the things they enjoyed.

Essy had never seen the appeal of jewelry. Even her wedding ring, a simple silver band, had lasted only until her pregnancy weight gain had given her a reason to take it off.

The ring had lived in her jewelry box, a mostly empty wooden box, from then on. It was probably still there. Essy had packed away the jewelry box along with a few of her husband's toys she couldn't stand to give away. Had the mechanical fur ball been one of the toys she kept? Essy couldn't remember. She hadn't been quite sane when she'd had to go through her home and decide what stayed and what went.

In the old science fiction show, the purring balls of fluff had soothed the captain's crew. The kitten seemed to be having the same effect on Essy. She hadn't thought of her wedding ring in ages. Hadn't been able to think of the fun she used to have with her husband without being overwhelmed by his absence.

"You give good purr," she said, scritching the kitten under its chin. "Snuggles."

It wasn't until later that night that she realized she'd given the kitten a name.

A week later Essy went back to the pet store for another bag of kitten food. It had taken the city four days to clear the streets enough for Essy to get her car out of the driveway and down to the intersection. More snow was forecast for the following week. While she had enough food to last her for weeks if she was snowed in again, which looked entirely possible, she didn't want to run out of food for Snuggles.

The owner had decorated her store for the holidays. An artificial tree stood inside the front door. One of the store's cats, a bob-tailed calico, was playing beneath the bottom branches, batting one of the low-hanging ornaments. Higher up the tree was decorated with handmade paper cutouts of dogs and cats. Each ornament bore a name: Feather, Wriggles, Hodgie, Noodles.

"That's our angel tree," the owner said. "Those ornaments all represent rescue animals. I thought it would be nice if I could generate a few donations to keep the rescue operation going for a while longer."

Essy frowned. Everyone was having money troubles. Even an all-volunteer organization needed money to feed and care for the animals it rescued.

She took the ornament for Feather. "How much?"

The owner smiled at her. "Whatever you want to give."

Essy added forty dollars to the bill for the kitten food. The owner didn't comment on Essy's purchase. Instead she handed Essy a photograph of a full grown cat, a white kitty with a brown tabby tail and a Siamese shaped face. The cat had vivid green eyes, and a pink nose and pink-tinged ears. "Feather," the owner said.

"She's beautiful," Essy said. She tried to hand the photograph back, but the owner wouldn't take it.

"Keep it," the owner said. "Unlike traditional angel trees, we want you to see who you're helping."

Essy took the photograph home and showed it to Snuggles. The kitten was far more interested in the bag of food. Essy had also purchased a small, covered plastic tub at the grocery store just to put the kitten's food in. Snuggles had already shredded a roll of toilet paper. Essy didn't want it learning how to hunt its own food by shredding the bag.

After she refilled Snuggles' dish, she put the picture of Feather on the mantel. It was the only photograph in the room. Essy didn't need pictures to remember what her husband and daughter had looked like.

"Our Christmas angel," she said.

Essy woke from a bad dream, heart pounding. The wind was howling outside and the kitten was crying at her bedroom door.

She had resisted letting the kitten in her bedroom. Most nights it fell asleep on the sofa, curled into a ball on one of the afghans Essy had made, and in the morning it would be waiting outside the door to Essy's bedroom. Tonight it was yelping for her. Loud, scared cries like it hadn't made since the first day Essy had found it in the snow.

Essy tried to turn on her bedroom light but nothing happened. The wind must have blown a transformer somewhere. When she threw back the covers, she was shocked at how cold it was in her house. No wonder the kitten was crying.

She kept a flashlight in her nightstand. She flicked it on and followed the beam to her door. The kitten bolted inside as soon as Essy opened the door, then stood blinking up at the light. Its eyes had been turning from baby blue to a rich, olive green. Both eyes were open wide, the pupils little more than slits.

"Come here, baby," Essy said, bending over to pick the kitten up.

In its fright, it sunk all its claws into her arm.

Essy winced. Sudden, unexpected tears welled in her eyes, and anger, white hot, consumed her.

Why did everything have to hurt? Hadn't she been through enough? What did the universe want from her?

Couldn't everything and everyone just leave her the hell alone?

When she looked down at the kitten, just for a moment she saw her daughter's cat. Heard her daughter say, "She didn't mean to hurt you, Mom. She's just scared of the wind."

Essy dropped the flashlight. Her daughter's voice had been as clear in her head as if they'd been in the same room.

Essy stumbled back against the bed. Icy snow beat against her bedroom window. Essy held the frightened kitten against her chest. She felt blood drip down her arm. Her back ached, her head ached, her arms ached to hold her family one more time. Just one more time.

They'd gone to the mall. Christmas shopping, just the three of them. It always had been just the three of them. Even after her daughter graduated from high school, she kept living at home while she went to a local college. Essy had married her high school sweetheart and become best friends with her daughter. The last thing she'd thought the day they went shopping was that she'd never get to hold her family again.

But a simple trip to the mall had changed all that. The man hadn't meant to destroy Essy's family. He didn't even know them. Enraged at being fired right before Christmas, he'd taken a gun into the department store where he'd worked and began shooting.

Her husband's attempt to shield his family had only been partially successful. Their daughter died on the way to the hospital. Essy's husband was pronounced dead at the scene, one of seven people the gunman killed that day before he turned the gun on himself.

Her daughter's blood had splattered Essy's arm, but the only injuries Essy had were the scratches her daughter's cat had made the night before when the wind had scared it so badly it had bolted over Essy where she sat on the sofa before tearing its way upstairs to her daughter's room. The cat had died from kidney failure six months after the shooting at the mall. Essy had been alone ever since.

She hadn't allowed herself to think about that day for years. She'd locked it away just like she'd locked away the Christmas ornaments and her wedding ring. She spent every holiday season hiding from a world where bad things happened to innocent people. If not for the kitten, she wouldn't have ventured out this year. Wouldn't have opened her heart up.

She'd made herself safe, but she'd made herself cold. Would that be what they'd want for her?

The future she'd wanted was gone, but she still had a future. Didn't she?

The kitten squirmed in her hands and cried at her. It was still scared.

"I'm sorry," she said. "You've come to live with a crazy person. I guess neither of us like dark, stormy nights."

Essy sniffled. She hadn't realized she'd been crying. How long had that been? She hadn't cried since the funeral.

She managed to get up off the floor. She took the kitten back to bed with her. Instead of nestling against her neck, it wriggled beneath the covers. Essy thought of one of the other names on the pet store's angel tree. Wriggles. Silly name for a pet.

"Like Snuggles is all that great," Essy said.

That was something her daughter would have said. Or her husband. They'd both been good at teasing her. She missed teasing.

She missed a lot of things. Maybe it was time to change all that.

Her old wedding ring still felt odd on Essy's finger. Slim and cold and strangely heavy for such a small thing. Essy couldn't seem to stop touching it with her thumb. If the owner of the pet food store noticed, she didn't say anything.

"I'd like to take this one too," Essy said, handing the owner the angel ornament for Wriggles along with forty dollars in cash.

In return, the owner handed Essy a photograph of a dog. A pug. In the picture the dog's tail was a blur, and Essy understood how the dog must have gotten its name.

"You sure you don't want to just adopt the real thing?" the owner asked.

Essy still thought one pet was enough for her, at least for now. She didn't want to become the crazy cat lady who lived in the house at the end of the block.

"I would like to volunteer, though," Essy said. "Sometime after the first of the year."

"You want to become a foster?"

Essy didn't know if she could do that. Take a pet into her house knowing it wouldn't be there long. "I'm not sure. Isn't there something else I could do?"

The store owner smiled at her. "I'll be happy to find out and let you know the next time you come in. Would that work for you?"

Essy told her it would. When she got to the door, she turned around and wished the woman a Merry Christmas. She wasn't sure who was more surprised.

When Essy got home, Snuggles met her at the door, then bounded away. Essy smiled. Kitten legs couldn't be made of bone, there had to be springs and rubber bands in there.

After she'd hung up her coat, Essy took the picture of Wriggles over to the tree. It had been hard work getting the artificial tree home from the store and setting it up single handed, not to mention hauling the plastic tub of ornaments down from the attic, but Essy was pleased with the end result. The tree didn't smell the same as the fresh pine trees her family used to have, but the artificial tree was less to fuss over. The old ornaments looked good on it, and so far Snuggles hadn't seemed inclined to climb the branches.

Essy had already hung the picture of Feather on the tree. She added the picture of the pug dog with the hyperactive tail. Her Christmas angels.

Something bounced off her ankle. Essy looked down and saw the loofa cat toy. Snuggles sat at her feet, looking up at her.

Essy picked up the toy and tossed it halfway across the living room. Snuggles raced after it. She half-expected the kitten to bring it back to her, but instead Snuggles scaled her husband's chair and dropped his prize next to the toy fur ball Essy had found in the attic along with her jewelry box.

She still had a ways to go, Essy knew that. She'd had a few rough moments unwrapping the ornaments, but she'd made it through. She'd keep making it through. For some reason she was still here. That reason might be as small as rescuing a stray kitten from a snowstorm, or there might be something else she was supposed to do. Whatever it was, Essy was pretty sure it didn't involve locking herself away from the world.

The tree was a start. She couldn't listen to any of her holiday music, not yet, but maybe next year. She might even put out some lights then. Something with color. Her neighbor's yard was pretty but it was cold. Essy'd had enough cold to last her a lifetime.

LOVE AMONG THE LLAMAS

Yesterday morning, I got in my car at seven twenty-five, same as always. I popped in a CD—*The Best of the Doobie Brothers* this time—and cranked up the volume to keep me awake, same as always. I stopped by Starbucks for a grande decaf latte, same as always. Took the freeway to where I-80 merges with Interstate 395, that grand old mess of looped interchanges and exits Reno locals call the Spaghetti Bowl. Same as always.

Only not quite.

Instead of veering right and taking the next off ramp, a left at the light three blocks down, and a right two blocks over into the parking garage, I stayed in the left lane and kept on driving east on the interstate.

And just like that, I quit my job.

Crazy, huh? Maybe I always was crazy and nobody ever noticed.

I had plenty of time after that to think about what I was doing. Once you get past Sparks going east on I-80, there's a whole lot of nothing but empty road since all the early morning traffic's going the other way. All those cars carrying commuters to their jobs, and none of them was me.

My heart hammered in my chest there for a while, let me tell you. I almost turned around at the next two off ramps I passed. But what was I leaving behind, really? An almost-empty apartment. A barren love life. A dead-end job for someone who'd only notice me by my absence.

I giggled a little about that. I could just imagine my boss's face when I didn't show at eight. At five after, he'd be checking his watch. By ten after, he'd be growing frantic.

At eight-fifteen, my cell phone rang.

I threw the phone out my car window—I didn't have an iPhone, just some cheap thing I got at Walmart—which only made me giggle harder. Bye-bye old life, hello you wide new wonderful world full of possibilities, you.

Of course, this part of that wonderful new world of possibilities was more of the same old, same old. Dry, sagebrush-filled, hot-as-hell in the summer and freezing cold in the winter. Nevada was a desert state. I should know. I'd been born here. I used to think the place was ugly, what with all that dry dirt, but yesterday morning, with golden, early-in-the-day sunshine streaming through my windshield, the world just felt different. I didn't know where I was going, where I'd stop, or what I'd do tomorrow. I figured I'd just drive until I got tired, had to pee, or I ran across something interesting.

As it turned out, I stopped when all three things happened almost at once.

Although, to be fair—the llama was what really made me stop.

I'd seen horses up close. Cows, too, and even sheep, but I'd never been nose to nose—or nose to neck—with a llama. But there, on the outskirts of Hazen, Nevada, a town that was little more than a blip on the road, I saw the words "Lighting Llamas" engraved onto a huge, curving sign over a rutted gravel driveway.

I pulled off the road and stopped beneath the sign. I rolled my window down and tried to decide if I wanted to get out of the car. I mean, there was a llama *right there* in the pasture next to the sign. Big, brown eyes, long eyelashes, creamy ivory fur. All I had to do was get out of the car, but for some reason I couldn't make myself do it.

The cicadas in the sagebrush on the other side of the road were buzzing up a storm. The day was already hot with the promise of getting nothing but hotter, and here I was, heading south in a car whose air-conditioning was spotty at best. What in the world had I been thinking?

I'm not sure why I turned off I-80 at Fernley except I had some vague notion about driving to Las Vegas, but now that I'd actually stopped driving, the whole idea seemed insane. It wasn't like I'd had any recent trauma, any life-changing event that made me want to chuck it all and start over. I had two credit cards to my name and just enough in my bank account to pay rent next month. I wasn't some heiress off on a wild adventure. I wasn't a secret witness skipping town. I was just a woman in her late twenties—okay, okay, twenty-nine, are you happy?—who was tired of her everyday life.

But had my everyday life been so bad? Maybe if I turned around and went home, called my boss and told him I'd overslept because I had a migraine, he wouldn't fire me.

Right. And there really is a Santa Claus, Virginia.

"I am so screwed," I said to no one in particular.

I about jumped out of my skin when someone answered me.

"Could be worse," a male voice said. "Doesn't look like you've got a flat, and your engine's still running. You ain't having a baby in there, are you?"

"No!" Good lord, no. You have to have a boyfriend—or at least a man with a working organ and a willingness to use it—to have a baby.

I craned my head around and saw the owner of the voice standing near the back of my car. My heart quit pumping double time out of fear and started thumping for a whole new reason.

If I'd been a Hollywood casting director looking for the next Sam Elliott lookalike for the next big budget Western (do they still make Westerns anymore?), I could have stopped my search right then. The guy was tall but not too tall, lanky but a strong-looking kind of lanky, with a craggy face that looked ruggedly handsome rather than old and worn out. He had on a cowboy hat (of course), but the hair beneath it was wavy brown shot through with the beginnings of what I imagined would be a full head of steel grey hair when he hit sixty. He had a thick moustache and his chin looked like he hadn't shaved in a couple of days. He had on a well-worn blue plaid shirt and faded jeans, and (of course, again) dusty cowboy boots.

"Well, that's good," he said, his smile digging deeper crags into his face. "I ain't never delivered a baby before. Not if it don't have four legs and a powerful long neck, at any rate."

He was talking about llamas. "Is this your place?" I asked. I wasn't sure if a the place where a person raised llamas was called a ranch or a farm, and I didn't want to insult him.

He nodded at me. "That it is." I heard the *Little Lady* even though he didn't say it. Good lord, the guy really was right out of Central Casting.

I frowned at him. "You're putting me on, right? Do you really talk that way, or is it just something the tourists expect?"

His eyes widened for a minute, then he looked at the ground at his feet. I heard him chuckle. "Okay," he said. "You got me."

I knew it! Sure, I didn't know how I knew it, but I did.

When he looked back up, he was still grinning, but he had color that didn't come from the sun in those rugged cheeks.

"Hope you don't hold it against me," he said. "But not a lot of people stop out here." He shrugged. "I'm hoping to make something out of this place someday. I'm still trying out the patter."

"No problem," I said. After all, I was trying out a new life, too. Sort of. If I didn't chicken out and go running back to my old one.

The second of my reasons for stopping made a sudden appearance. I'd polished off my decaf latte before I hit the Fernley exit, and now I needed a bathroom. In a hurry.

"Hey, is there a place around here where I can use a restroom?" I asked. I hadn't seen a gas station or fast food place since Fernley. I really should have stopped there and taken care of things, but I wasn't exactly thinking straight.

"Nearest gas station is ten miles back toward town."

Ten miles. I didn't think I could make ten miles.

He must have seen the hesitation on my face.

"Or you could come up to the house," he said. "I promise I'm not a llama-raising serial killer."

"Sure you're not," I said. "Isn't that what all serial killers would say?"

"Except for Dexter. He'd admit it."

That he would. *Dexter* was one of my favorite—

"Hey, wait!" I said. "You watch *Dexter*?"

"Satellite dish," he said. "When you live out in the middle of nowhere, it helps to have cable. Or the equivalent."

Huh.

My bladder twinged. Good grief. It was either the llama-rancher's bathroom or go pee behind a clump of sagebrush and hope I didn't run into a rattlesnake. Why, again, had I thought driving across the Nevada desert in the middle of the day without any kind of provisions or plan or even a change of clothes was a good idea?

"Lead the way," I said.

It turned out the llama rancher had a dusty old pickup truck, no surprise, but his ranch house looked like any other suburban house I'd ever been in.

"It's pretty new," he said to me. "I've got a buddy who's a developer in Fernley. He was doing pretty good until the housing market went bust, so I hired him to build me a new place. What do you think?"

"I think I'm back in Reno," I said. But in an upscale neighborhood. The house had high ceilings and spacious rooms, tiled floors, and a magnificent view of the desert landscape out of floor-to-ceiling windows in the living room. Even the bathroom was upscale, with an open area shower instead of a walled-in stall or a dinky little tub.

And that was the guest bathroom.

I tried not to snoop too much while I used his bathroom. The place was surprisingly neat for a man's house. Not that all men were slobs, but I didn't think most men kept a scented candle on a holder in their guest bathroom. I sighed. He was either gay or married, and either option left me feeling more disappointed than I should have been. After all, I was just passing through, and the only reason I'd stopped was for the llamas, right?

Of which I'd only seen the one.

My Sam Elliott lookalike llama rancher was in the living room when I got done. "So where do you keep the rest of your llamas?" I asked. I'd followed his truck down a rutted dirt road nearly a half mile before I realized it was his driveway. The fields on both sides of the driveway had sheep in them, but no llamas that I could see.

"The rest?"

"The sign did say Lighting Llamas," I said. "Not Lightning Llama."

He nodded at me and grinned. "Got me there." He gestured toward the bank of windows. "There's another field out back, over that little rise. I have four llamas back there, a male and three females. This time next year I hope to have seven."

I tried to see a boundary fence and realized I couldn't. "How much land do you have here?"

"A little over eighty acres."

Wow.

"And you live here all alone?"

I'd peeked inside his medicine cabinet—I couldn't help myself—and there hadn't been anything feminine on the shelves. No eye shadow, no lipstick, no makeup of any kind. Not that that meant anything. I mean, it was the guest bathroom.

His grin turned into a full-out smile, the kind of slow smile that said he knew I'd peeked and he wasn't upset about it.

"Yup," he said. "Hazen's not exactly a hot spot for meeting women, and I work too hard to make the drive into Fernley more than once or twice a month. The only reason I saw you down by the highway today was because I was riding the fence line, checking for breaks."

He was standing pretty close to me now, but I wasn't picking up any serial killer vibes. The vibes I was getting were all first-date nerves type of vibes.

Not that I'd been on a first date in a long time, but I dimly remembered the feeling, and I was pretty sure this was it.

"You check the fence line in your truck? I thought ranchers rode a horse to do that."

He chuckled. He had a nice chuckle, I decided.

"You've seen too many movies," he said. "Truck's faster and I don't have to clean up after it."

"Good point."

He tilted his head a little to look at me like he was giving me a serious once-over. I couldn't quite read his expression yet, but I liked whatever expression it was I saw in his hazel eyes.

"You're not like any other woman I've ever met," he said finally.

"Because I like *Dexter*?"

"Nope." He drew just a little closer. "Because you stopped to see my llamas, and you haven't complained once about only seeing the one."

True. Of course, right about now llamas were the last thing on my mind. The first thing on my mind was how nice he smelled, even though he'd been out in the heat in a battered old truck, and the next thing was how I'd been wrong all along when I thought he might be gay. Definitely not gay, not if the way he was studying my mouth was any indication.

As we stood there, I realized he wasn't going to make a move without a little effort on my part, so I leaned forward just the tiniest bit.

I don't know where I got the courage or the knowledge. My love life has never been what you'd call exciting or even vaguely adventurous, but here I was, in a strange man's house out in the middle of the desert, and I wasn't the least bit concerned he'd go all serial killer on me.

Yes, I most definitely had gone crazy.

That thought was wiped out of my mind when he kissed me.

It wasn't a grand, passionate kiss that swept us both off our feet, nor was it an electric zing kind of a kiss that left me breathless. No, it was a perfect gentlemanly kiss, just enough pressure of his lips to let me know I'd been kissed, and enough of a brush of his mustache to tickle. He didn't touch me except with his lips, and before I knew it, the kiss was over.

I opened my eyes and looked into his. "That was nice," I said.

He gave me an *aw, shucks* smile. "Yes, ma'am."

I felt like punching him in the shoulder—a friendly punch, mind you—but I held off as something occurred to me. "What's your name?" I asked. I'd never kissed someone before whose name I didn't know.

"Chet," he said.

"Kate," I said, feeling like I should hold out my hand for a shake. I managed to control the urge. A stronger one was taking its place. An urge to carry on with the kissing, and carry on soon.

Chet backed away from me, and I felt a sharp twinge of disappointment. It disappeared when he reached up to tuck a strand of my hair behind my ear. "So," he said. "How would you like to go meet the rest of my llamas?"

As a follow-up to a kiss, "meeting Mr. Right's llamas" was definitely not part of the dating handbook. I didn't care. This day was all about doing things outside the norm.

"I'd love to," I said.

Chet's llamas were the coolest things I'd ever seen. I even got to pet them, although Chet warned me that llamas, just like camels, tended to spit. I supposed I was lucky. None of them did.

After we finished communing with the llamas, we drove back to the house and Chet fixed me lunch. He made ham and cheese on rye, which tasted like heaven considering it had been a while since my meager before-work granola bar and latte. We took our time eating, and I got to hear about how Chet had inherited the ranch from a great uncle.

"He was Basque," Chet said. "He'd had this sheep ranch going out here for something like forty years. Never made a lot of money, just enough to keep himself from going under. His wife died twenty years before he did. I used to come visit when I was little. I was the only one of the kids in my generation who did, so I guess that's why he left it to me."

"Did he have llamas, too?"

Chet shook his head. "That's something I brought in. I'd heard that llamas were good at keeping the coyotes away from sheep, so I bought a couple. Then I found out gelded males made the best watch llamas. Well, by then I had another little llama on the way, and I just couldn't bring myself to do that to the little bugger, so I decided to raise them instead. That's when I got the idea for naming the place 'Lightning Llamas,' but so far you're my first guest."

I ate the last bite of sandwich. "You're a wonderful host for a man who doesn't get much company."

He was looking at me like he had after we'd kissed. I reached across the corner of the dining room table and took his hand.

"So tell me, Kate. Where are you heading?"

I felt a little embarrassed by my early morning decision to chuck my life out the window and just drive, but he'd told me about his life, so I told him about my morning. When I was done, his eyebrows were climbing his forehead, and he let out a low whistle.

"I'm impressed," he said.

"You are?"

"My friends thought I was nuts to give up what I had to move out here and raise sheep for a living."

"What were you doing before?"

He chuckled. "Selling copiers. Never did quite seem to fit. I'm guessing your life didn't fit you, either."

No, it didn't. "I think realizing I'd been going through the motions—the same exact motions—every day, day in and day out, finally did me in. I just couldn't do it one more day."

He looked down at where I still held his hand. "You didn't answer my question, though."

"I didn't?"

"Nope." He took a deep breath. "Where were you heading when you decided to stop here?"

"Originally? Vegas. But I'd just about talked myself into going back. I guess you could said I was at kind of a crossroads."

"Crossroads at the Lightning Llama. Sounds like the title for a bad Western."

"Or a bad romance," I said, then wished I hadn't when he gently took his hand away and stood up from the table.

"Well, I guess you better get a move on, then," he said. "Vegas is still a pretty good drive from here."

He took our dishes into the kitchen. I hesitated for a moment, then followed him.

"Did I do something wrong?" I asked.

He stood at the sink, rinsing the dishes off and not looking at me. "I'm too old to do casual," he said. "You've got your whole life in front of you. Me, I'm making a second life for myself out here. It's not much, but I enjoy it. I want to keep on enjoying it after you leave, you understand?"

Oddly enough, I did. In fact, the more I thought about it, I decided that was another reason I'd pointed my car east and just drove. I was tired of living in a place where I waited by the phone for my first dates to call back for a second, or where I ate take-out by myself, or watched television alone.

"You know," I said, walking over to the sink. "We both like *Dexter*. We both turned our backs on a life that wasn't working. And your llamas didn't spit at me. That's gotta mean something, right?"

He grinned and shook his head. "You're something else, you know?" He let the soapy water swirl down the drain and turned to face me. "You trying to tell me something?"

I grinned back. "I didn't have my heart set on Vegas. All I told myself was that I'd drive until I found something interesting or I had to pee." I didn't think I should tell him about the tired part. "I thought the llamas were the interesting thing, then I met you." I touched his shoulder. "Good romances have started with less."

"Merely good?"

This time I was the one who chuckled. "Okay, great. Great romances."

He leaned forward, and this time he kissed me like he meant it.

We went to bed after that, of course, where we did a great many things like we meant it. Chet didn't ask me to stay. He didn't have to. We'd already settled that issue in the kitchen, and besides, his bed was about the most comfortable thing I'd ever slept in. It probably had something to do with the fact that he was in it.

The next morning I didn't have a Starbucks decaf grande latte. I'm pretty sure there's not a Starbucks within thirty miles of Chet's ranch, and besides, Chet makes pretty good decaf himself. I didn't listen to the Doobie Brothers in my car. I did call my boss—my former boss—on Chet's cell phone to let the man know I wasn't dead, I just wasn't coming back ever again. He told me not to bother, I was fired. I think we both hung up on each other. It seemed a fitting way to leave that job behind.

Chet did tell me I should go back and get my things, and that he'd be happy to do that with me. We're going to make the drive to Reno tomorrow. Today I'm going with him while he finishes checking his fence line, then the rest of the day we're spending in bed. Chet says he's old and can't spend the entire day in bed with me because I'd probably kill him. I think he's being melodramatic. He's no slouch in the bedroom department, gray or no gray in his hair.

I never thought, in all my wildest dreams, that I'd end up on a llama ranch outside of Hazen, but it's a future I can see for myself now. Most people would tell me to take it slow, but I've been taking it slow all my life. Doing the things everyone expected me to do for so long that I'd begun to expect that's all my life would ever be. Why take it slow when you know what you're doing is right? And why keeping doing stuff that you know is wrong just because that's what you've always done?

Yeah, I don't have any good answers to those questions either, and the beauty of it is I don't need any. I found my happily ever after where I least expected it.

I do have one question, though.

What are we going to name the baby llamas?

NAMES IN THE SAND

Cissy wrapped her leather jacket more firmly around her shoulders and tried not to think about what the wind was doing to her hair. She'd saved up for months for a trip to the beach. She'd be damned if the cold snap was going to stop her from enjoying the sound of the surf and the sea birds, and the laughter of the few brave kids out on the sand playing keep-away with the waves.

At least the sun was out, not that it was doing all that much good to keep her warm. She'd dressed in layers, something menopausal women learned to do for self-preservation against unexpected hot flashes. She could use a good hot flash right about now.

Even with the leather jacket on top of her windbreaker on top of her sweatshirt on top of her blouse, she was still freezing. If she didn't warm up soon, she'd have to give up staring at the ocean from behind the concrete retaining wall that separated the parking lot from the beach a good ten feet below, and go watch the waves from the warmth of her car.

The kids on the beach didn't seem to feel the cold. Cissy

watched a new group of teenagers—two girls and three boys—tramp across the sand wearing nothing but shorts and tee shirts. The boys were carrying boogie boards, the girls beach towels. Wires trailed down from their ears to whatever MP3 players they had stuffed in their pockets. Cissy wondered if they even heard the sound of the waves over whatever music was popular with teenagers these days.

Someone had written a name in the sand—SPENCER—stomped out in huge, rambling letters above the high tide mark. The teenagers walked right through the letters, smearing the S and the tail of the P and taking the top off the E and the N before they headed down toward the waves, leaving the rest of the name alone.

What a shame. Someone had gone to a lot of trouble to leave his name in the sand in a spot where the waves wouldn't obliterate it.

For a moment Cissy thought about going down to the beach and fixing the smeared letters, but her legs gave her trouble these days, and slogging through dry sand would make her calves ache for days. Poor Spencer, whoever he'd been, would have to settle for semi-posterity, at least until more children and teenagers and careless adults scuffed through his name entirely.

If Harry was still alive, he would have fixed the letters for her. Harry would have done anything for her, and he had for nearly thirty years.

He'd even sat by her side on innumerable park benches and picnic benches and glider swings, nose buried in a book or snoring quietly behind dark glasses, while Cissy sat and enjoyed the outdoors, no matter where that outdoors happened to be. Sometimes she brought her crocheting with her, and sometimes she brought a book or a camera, but most of the time she just sat and watched the world go on around her.

This late spring visit to the Oregon coast was the first trip Cissy had taken since Harry passed away last November.

Her friends thought she was nuts to make the trip by herself. Amanda was certain Cissy's car would break down in some back roads town and she'd be set upon by thieves who'd think a middle-aged woman traveling alone was easy pickings. Nora thought Cissy would attract the attention of "unsavory types," which in Nora's book was anyone who didn't have six figures in a money market account and houses on both coasts with a condo or two somewhere in the middle.

Cissy's daughter was the only one who had simply wished Cissy a good time.

"Have fun, Mom," she'd said, her voice scratchy over the old cell phone Cissy refused to replace with one of the new smart phone models. "You deserve it."

Cissy wasn't so sure about that. How could a woman who'd wished for her husband's death have fun living the rest of her life without him?

A crow landed on the iron railing on top of the retaining wall a few feet to Cissy's left. The crow gave her a good look with one eye, probably sizing her up as a potential good Samaritan who carried spare food in her pocket.

"You're out of luck," she said to the bird.

She never fed the birds. She'd seen Alfred Hitchcock's movie when she was a little girl, and she took it as a cautionary tale.

Off to her right, she heard a man chuckle. "I don't think he'll be discouraged that easy."

Cissy turned her head to look at the man who'd laughed at her and the bird.

She'd been aware of him when he'd sat down on the concrete bench, just like she was aware of everyone around her—being cautious, as her mother would have said—but she hadn't given him a second look. She wasn't really here to meet people, only to spend time at the beach.

He was sixty if he was a day. His skin was a mottled olive tan, but a faded version of itself, like he was a man whose family hailed from the Mediterranean but who'd lived his life in a city crowded with tall buildings where the sun never reached street level.

His accent had its roots in the deep South. His "I" had come out "ah," and the words were rich and slow. His hair was steel grey salted with white, long and thick and tied at the nape of his neck with a strip of leather. He had on dark-lensed sunglasses, and his beard had been trimmed into a neat little moustache and goatee. He wore a heavy leather coat like Cissy, only his was the scuffed brown of a bomber jacket while hers was black suede. He wore jeans like she did, and brown leather boots where she wore sneakers.

"He can come and go as he pleases," Cissy said, referring to the crow. "I just didn't want to get his hopes up."

The man chuckled again. "That's a good attitude to have around birds."

He got up from the bench and leaned on the iron rail at the top of the retainer wall.

Cissy was pleased he hadn't tried to come any closer to her. She didn't mind talking to strangers, but she had no intention of letting any of them get within grabbing distance. She had a small can of pepper spray in her jacket pocket to back up her intentions. Amanda would have been proud.

The crow tilted its head at her, then flapped its wings and flew out over the sand, no doubt looking for that good Samaritan. Cissy wished it well.

"You know," the man from the South said. "There's a great deal of mythology built up around that bird."

"That particular bird?" Cissy asked.

"Maybe," the man said, drawing the word out. "But I meant crows in general more than that one bird in particular, although he did seem very smart."

Cissy waited for the man to make some remark about how the crow was smart because it chose her, which she imagined would be the man's next line if his intent was to "hit on" her, as Cissy's daughter might say.

Not that Cissy expected any man to hit on her. She wasn't a classic beauty, more of the sturdy, handsome type, not that she'd ever appreciated that term as it was used to describe women. Men were handsome; women were pretty, or pleasant-looking, or simply not ugly.

Cissy would settle for not ugly. Her hair was thinning and had entirely too much white in the formerly blonde curls for the result to be described as salted. Rather, in her case the entire salt shaker had been dumped upside down on top of her head since that's where the white hair had taken root in its conquest of the blonde.

She had wrinkles on her forehead from too much time spent frowning, and her eyes still showed signs of the tension of the last few years in the myriad of tiny creases at the corners of her eyelids. The blue of her eyes was fading, and the whites were no longer as clear as they'd been when she was a young girl. She wore no makeup to hide the imperfections the years had left on her skin. She was simply who she was—a fifty-four year old widow who expected to live the rest of her life alone.

Instead of saying something flirtatious, the man said, "Hindus, Buddhists, Japanese, and Chinese all think crows are special, although the reasons why have not always been flattering."

Cissy remembered a series of movies her daughter used to watch. In those movies, the crow had been a symbol of the avenging dead.

She shivered, and not entirely from the cold wind blowing off the water.

Cissy didn't consider herself a superstitious person, and besides, Harry didn't have any reason to seek vengeance. His foe had been cancer and pain and the long, slow wasting away that came from being trapped inside a body intent on killing him long before his time.

Something must have shown on her expression. The man stood up a little straighter, and a frown creased a line in between his bushy eyebrows.

He didn't need to take off his sunglasses for Cissy to know his eyes would have the same expression that had been in all her friends' eyes until she'd finally told them to quit treating her like she was made of glass. Women survived their husbands all the time and got on with life just fine. Cissy would, too.

"I've hit a bad subject," the man said. "I'm so sorry. It's not what I intended."

The deep South in his speech gave the words greater impact. Cissy felt an irrational urge to bow her head in graceful acceptance of his apology.

"No need to apologize," she said instead, her voice coming out gruffer than she intended. "There's no way you could have known."

"I could have guessed." He nodded at her hands where they rested on the railing. "You still wear your ring, but you've been out here by yourself for nearly an hour. You're clearly just visiting."

Cissy raised her eyebrows at that. How could he know? Even if he'd seen her park her car, it was a rental she'd picked up at the airport in Portland, and it had an Oregon state license plate.

"The locals aren't as intrigued with simply watching the ocean as we tourists are," he said to her unasked question. "To them, the ocean's simply a part of the landscape."

She smiled a little. She'd never thought of the ocean as simple in any way, shape, or form. To her, the vastness of it alone made the ocean special.

"How do you know my husband's not just taking a nap at the motel?"

"That's true, I don't. But in my experience, couples on vacation usually do things together."

"Or they take separate vacations."

"Did you and your husband ever take separate vacations?" the man asked.

Cissy had to think about it. Harry had traveled for work and so had she, but a vacation? There'd been so few true vacations, most of them when their daughter was little. After she'd grown up and moved out on her own and the two of them finally had time to travel, that had been the time Harry first got ill and they couldn't.

"No," she said, and she looked back out over the water.

The last time she'd been on this beach, her daughter had been ten. The three of them had driven down the coast almost the entire length of the state of Oregon. They'd picked up Highway 101 at Astoria, Washington, and driven the windy coast road through small town after small town, surprised at the number of Dairy Queens they passed along the way, and stopped here and there at public beaches to stretch their legs.

They'd bought a teddy bear in a specialty shop and found this beach access a half mile down the road. Cissy had sat on a bench just a few feet away from where she now stood while Harry and their daughter slogged through the sand and looked for seashells. Not that they found many. The coast here was too rough for seashells to survive the surf intact, but Harry had brought Cissy a piece of white shell ground smooth as glass. She still had it in her jewelry box back home.

For a moment she could almost see Harry down there on the beach, bent over at the waist so he could peer through his glasses at the sand, looking for seashells.

Why in the world had she ever wanted him to die?

"He had cancer," she said to the man with the smooth Southern voice. "He was fifty-eight when he passed, and he was the only man I ever loved."

Harry had suffered terribly at the end. He'd asked her to help him leave, but she'd been a coward. She'd loved him, and all she could do for him was pray to whatever God might exist that He let her husband die.

She doubted she'd ever forgive herself for that.

On the beach below, the teenage boys emerged from the waves, lugging their boogie boards and dripping cold water on the girls where they lay on beach towels. The girls shrieked and scampered away, scuffing through the few unblemished letters in Spencer's name.

"Kids," Cissy said.

The man turned to look down at the beach. She felt relieved he was no longer looking at her. She could only take so much concern from total strangers.

"I don't think I was ever that young," the man said.

"I know I wasn't," Cissy said, relieved that he had accepted her change of subject.

They both watched the teenagers chase each other around the beach, boogie boards forgotten. Seagulls hovered nearby, more brazen than the crow in looking for a handout. Farther down the beach, a father was showing his young son how to fly a kite. The kid looked barely big enough to hang onto the thing in the strong wind.

Harry had never flown a kite as far as Cissy knew, but Harry wasn't with her on this vacation. This time around, she was on her own.

"Do you know anything about kites?" Cissy asked.

"Kites?"

The man with the Southern accent took his sunglasses off and perched them on top of his head. Cissy wasn't altogether surprised to see that his eyes were a soft, expressive brown.

"I've never flown one, and it seems to me that today is as good a time as any to learn."

There was a kite shop a block away on the other side of the highway. A convenient stop light made crossing the highway less of a risk to life and limb.

"I do believe I should like to try my hand at kite flying as well," the man with the Southern accent said. He stuck out his hand. "Theodore," he said. "Theodore Monroe."

Cissy hesitated before she took his hand and shook it. "Cecilia," she said.

Cissy had been Harry's name for her. Amanda always told her that Cissy wasn't a proper name for women their age, but Cissy hadn't cared.

She still didn't, not really, but for some reason, this man—Theodore—seemed like someone she should be Cecilia with, even if all they did was fly kites on the beach and then go their separate ways.

The kite shop was filled with such a wide array of kites Cissy had trouble choosing which one she wanted. She decided on a multi-colored kite in a traditional diamond shape. Theodore chose a slightly more elaborate model, and they both listened carefully to the clerk's instructions on how to fly them in the ocean wind.

As they made their way back to the beach, they passed the teenagers from the beach loading their gears into cars in the parking lot. The boys and the girls looked suitably cold, and Cissy found her faith in the order of the universe somewhat restored.

"You don't think we'll have to run to get these in the air, do you?" she asked Theodore. She didn't think her knees were up to running on sand.

He squinted as he turned his face into the wind, his sunglasses now safely tucked inside his shirt pocket. "I don't believe getting them airborne will be a problem. Keeping them there, now that will be the trick."

For someone who professed he'd never flown a kite, Theodore knew what he was talking about. Getting the kites off the ground proved to be easy. Keeping the things from dive-bombing the sand was another thing entirely.

Cissy lost track of time as she worked her kite, up and down and up again, followed by the inevitable downward dive, until finally she caught the breeze just right and the kite soared. She was surprised at the strength of the tug on her line and the sense of accomplishment she felt from so simple a thing as keeping the kite in the air.

"I did it!" she said. "I did it. Look at this, Ha—"

She stopped herself before she said the entire name.

If Theodore heard, he pretended not to. "You have done a magnificent job, while I, on the other hand, have failed miserably."

True. He hadn't been able to keep his kite in the air for more than a few moments at a time.

Her arms were starting to ache. She was unaccustomed to holding onto something high over her head for any length of time, but even with the ache in her arms and the building ache in her legs from walking on the sand, she was having fun. Truly, unexpectedly— she was having fun.

Why hadn't she ever done this before?

Why hadn't she come down on the sand, looked for seashells with Harry and their daughter, and run away from the waves?

Why had she spent her life just watching and never doing?

Spencer had written his name in the sand in great big letters. The letters wouldn't last, but nothing ever did. That didn't mean it wasn't worth doing.

Cissy pulled her kite down and reeled in the line.

"Ah, just as well," Theodore said, following suit. "I was beginning to embarrass myself in front of a lady."

Cissy shook her head. "No, I'm the one who should be embarrassed. I'm afraid I took advantage of your good nature." She shrugged. She didn't want to lead him on any more than she already had. "I'm not sure what you were expecting, but this is about all I'm good for."

Theodore looked at her with his expressive brown eyes. He had lines of his own at the corners of his eyes. She wasn't the only one who was out on the beach alone for a reason, but she had things she still had to come to terms with before she could even consider being there for someone else.

"I believe I understood that when you told me about your husband," he said. "You may not believe me, but I have had a wonderful time with you, Cecilia, and wonderful times are to be treasured, no matter how brief."

He didn't offer to shake her hand again, nor did he attempt to give her an awkward hug.

Instead he just gazed at her for a moment, then he nodded his head just the slightest bit, put on his sunglasses, and walked away.

Theodore didn't look back as he walked toward the parking lot, lugging his kite with him. Cissy wondered if he'd ever try to fly it again. She thought he might.

She looked down at the kite at her feet, and was surprised to discover she was standing in a straight line of footprints. She was standing in upstroke of Spencer's N, or what was left of it.

"Oh, Spencer," she said.

She could always redraw the letters. She'd be taking pain relievers that night anyway for all her kite-flying aches and pains. What was the difference if she added a few more?

Cissy retraced Spencer's name until the letters were clear once more. She backed away, regarding her handiwork. Not bad, even though the lines were a little narrower. Spencer, whoever he'd been, had big feet.

The layers of her blouse and sweatshirt, windbreaker and jacket were a little uncomfortable. She'd worked up a sweat. She hoped she hadn't worked up a hot flash. They came less often these days, but they hadn't gone away totally.

She turned her face into the wind to cool her skin. Her hair was probably a mess by now, all the grey and blonde mixed together in a rat's nest it would take a half hour or more to untangle.

She should cut her hair short like most women her age, but she'd always worn her hair long. Harry had liked it that way, said it made her look like a free spirit, not a cookie-cutter old married lady.

She never had been the adventurous, free-spirited type, not when she'd been married. She might not be adventurous ever again after she got done doing whatever it was she'd started by going on this journey, but that was okay. She liked who she'd been when she was Harry's wife. She wanted to like who she'd be as Harry's widow.

Her knees started to bark at her, the joints sore like she knew they'd be. She really should head back to her motel. She had a long drive ahead of her in the morning. She planned to take the rental car all the way up the coast to Astoria, but she had one more thing she wanted to do now.

She walked a little way down the beach until she came to a flat area above the high tide line where the sand was dry.

The walking was harder here, but she didn't mind. If Spencer could do it, so could she.

She took her bearings and then started shuffling a path in the sand the width of her two feet. She kept walking until she'd made a line.

A long upstroke.

The left side of the letter H.

and for more from Annie Reed...

an excerpt from the
opening pages of

A Death
in
Cumberland

a Jill Jordan mystery

CHAPTER ONE

Nora Corbitt parked her car at the very edge of the dirt parking lot at Founders Park. The lot was full, but at this time of night no one would see her back here so close to the street.

The two baseball diamonds on the far side of the lot were lit so bright it looked like the middle of the day over there, but the banks of lights were focused on the playing fields, and the parking lot didn't have any lights of its own. Where Nora stood next to her car, she was hidden by the long shadows thrown by the few spindly trees that separated the lot from the baseball fields, and that was just the way she liked it.

It seemed like everyone in Cumberland had turned out for the city league tournament. Grown men playing softball like their lives depended on it.

She'd seen flyers for the tournament at the grocery store. Nora didn't like crowds, and she hated sports and the men who played them. She wouldn't have left her house at all except for the cat.

"I have this cat, it's a stray, but my dad won't let me keep it.

Can you take it? I hear you do that, right? Take in cats?"

The voice on the phone that afternoon had been young. Nora didn't trust the young, and she hadn't answered right away.

"I'm afraid my dad will kill it. He doesn't like cats."

Nora had stroked the calico in her lap, a beautiful cat with only one eye. The cat was like her, a survivor. That's all Nora had ever wanted to do—help the cats survive.

"Yes," she'd said to the young voice. "I can take it."

They'd arranged to meet in the parking lot at Founders Park. "After the games start. My dad will be playing and he won't notice if I'm gone for a few minutes."

Nora didn't ask why the meeting had to be secret. She'd lived in Cumberland long enough to know that people who lived in small towns had their secrets, just like the town itself had secrets. Nora was one of them.

A secret, or maybe just a past the town didn't want to remember.

That was fine with her. She didn't want to think about the past either, only unlike the town, she couldn't help it.

No one was waiting for her in the lot. She shouldn't have been surprised. Kids played pranks, and they seemed to play more than their fair share on her.

She shivered inside her jacket. She'd stood waiting by her car for too long. It was fall in Cumberland, and in northern Nevada the desert got cold after dark.

She should go home, let the calico climb on her lap again, and stroke the cat's pretty fur until they both fell asleep. The calico was the only cat Jeremiah let her keep in the house. It was too old now to do any damage to his furniture. Mostly it slept on Nora's bed. When she was home, it slept on her.

She opened her car door and was about to get inside when she heard a voice calling to her.

"Over here!"

The voice didn't sound as young in person. It came from the empty field on the other side of the parking lot.

Nora squinted but couldn't see anything in the gloom except dried-out cheatgrass, tall weeds, and a vague shape that looked like nothing more than a darker shadow.

"Bring the cat to me," she said, "or I'm leaving."

"I can't."

Nora stood by her car. The open door and the little dome light inside gave her a sense of security.

She could get in and lock the door before anyone came at her in the dark. She didn't want to go out in the field, not at night, not without a flashlight. Not alone, and she was always alone. Why hadn't she brought a flashlight?

"If you can't come get it, I'll just let it go out here. It'll be okay, right?"

"No! Don't do that."

Too many dogs lived in Cumberland, and their owners didn't keep them fenced in. Coyotes roamed the empty fields. She couldn't leave a cat out here. What if it had been someone's pet? What if it didn't know how to survive on its own?

"I'm coming," she said. "Just wait a minute."

Nora had a gun in her purse. She never traveled anywhere without it.

She got the gun and dropped it in the deep pocket of her jacket. She shut her car door but didn't lock it. She'd be able to run back to her car and lock herself inside if she needed to. Until then, she'd keep her hand on the gun in her pocket and everything would be fine.

Even after the gloom of the parking lot, the darkness of the field was nearly absolute. The ground beneath the tall, dry weeds was rocky and uneven.

If she just concentrated on putting one foot in front of the next, she would be all right. She'd take the cat and go back to her car. It would be scared, but she'd take care of it.

She could be strong for the cat. She was strong. She'd survived. She could do a simple thing like this. There was nothing to be frightened of. She had a gun. This time she had a gun.

The sharp *crack!* of a bat connecting solidly with a ball made her flinch. The crowd at the baseball field erupted in cheers.

The skin on Nora's neck crept up in gooseflesh. The night was too dark in this field, and she'd walked too far. She heard rustling in the field but she couldn't see the dark shape anymore. She needed to get back to her car.

"Bring me the cat," she said, dismayed but not surprised to hear the trembling in her voice.

"It's over here."

Now the voice was behind her.

How did it get behind her?

Nora whirled, dragging the gun out of her pocket.

Something solid connected with her hand just as she got a good grip on the gun.

The pain was enormous. Nora cried out as the gun went flying from her suddenly numb and useless fingers.

"You're so easy," the voice said, this time sounding not like a child at all.

She clutched her broken hand to her chest as her attacker laughed at her. The parking lot was on the far side of that laughter. She couldn't get there without being hit again.

She turned in the other direction and fled.

"That's right. Run!"

The uneven ground nearly made her stumble. Every stride sent electric, white hot jolts of pain through her injured arm. She lost a shoe in the dead weeds, and a rock bit into the flesh at the bottom of her foot, but she would have kept running if her ribs hadn't suddenly exploded in pain.

The force of the blow knocked her off her feet. She landed on her broken hand, and this time the pain was so horrible she nearly blacked out. She tried to scream but she couldn't get enough air in her lungs.

"Get up," her attacker said.

"Please." The word was little more than a whimper forced out through a red haze of pain.

"Get up!"

Nora did.

She managed only a few more shaky strides before another blow sent her sprawling.

The next blow came down on the back of her head.

Dirt and dry grass clogged her nose and got into her open mouth. A buzzing, ringing noise filled her head. She sputtered, trying to spit out the dirt. She couldn't get her legs to work. She tried to pull herself forward with her good hand, but her fingers scrabbled uselessly at the ground.

One more blow landed on her head, and the buzzing got so loud it had blotted out everything else. The dark night had given way to a tunnel of black so thick Nora felt like she was drowning in tar.

For a moment she saw the calico's sweet, one-eyed face in that blackness, saw the faces of all the cats she had ever loved and cared for and lost, but then they faded, too, even as her fingers stopped moving and her breathing slowed.

By the time the next blow fell, Nora Corbitt was dead.

CHAPTER TWO

Cliff & Mattie's Diner faced Main Street, Cumberland's name for Highway 50 where the lonely two-lane desert highway widened to four lanes for the mile and a half it passed through town.

Sixty miles southeast of Reno, Cumberland was the only town to speak of in Silverado County, the third largest county in Nevada.

Cumberland was also the Silverado county seat, and the place Sheriff Jill Jordan called home, along with some forty-eight hundred other permanent residents, an ever-shifting population of transients who lived on the outskirts of town, and the occasional traveler who wanted a place to stop and gas up on the way to either Reno or Las Vegas.

Travelers usually bypassed Cliff & Mattie's in favor of the $3.99 all-you-can-eat buffet at the Golden Nugget Hotel & Casino, only a half-mile down Main from the diner.

Locals preferred the homey atmosphere of Cliff & Mattie's. Everybody who was a regular knew everyone else, and gossip was served right alongside simple meals in ample portions. If anything of importance happened in Cumberland, all the regulars knew about it before the local newspaper even caught a whiff.

Gossip was the reason Sheriff Jill Jordan ate breakfast at Cliff & Mattie's five days a week, just like her father had. Charlie Jordan had been a patrol deputy. He'd taught his daughter at a young age that in order to protect and serve the public, an officer needed to get to know the citizens that officer served.

In Cumberland most gossip had just a big enough kernel of truth in it to give Jill an opportunity to stop small problems before they became official complaints.

Back in the days when Jill's father ate breakfast at the diner, the red leatherette booths had been new and soft, the cushions on the aluminum-edged stools at the counter still had enough padding to be comfortable, the black enamel on the tables and chairs had been new and unchipped, and the black-and-white checkerboard linoleum floor was slick and shiny.

The red leatherette in the booths had stiffened and cracked in a few places over the years, and the cushions on the stools weren't quite as comfortable, but Cliff & Mattie's would always be the heart of Cumberland.

On this October morning Jill took her usual seat at the end of the counter where it curved toward the hallway leading to the restrooms. The spot let her see the rest of the diner while she ate. It was also isolated enough to let her read the morning paper in peace if she wanted.

"Morning, Jill." Tina Williams, the morning waitress, set a small silver pot of hot water next to Jill's coffee cup. A bag of decaf Earl Grey tea lay on the white paper doily that decorated the saucer beneath the teapot. "Same as usual?"

Jill put down her paper next to the place setting. "Yeah, thanks." She dipped the teabag in the hot water. Decaf Earl Grey wasn't coffee, but her doctor said it was better for Jill's blood pressure.

Tina was a divorced mom like Jill, but ten years younger. Tina

ANNIE REED

had a good figure and what Jill thought of as Loretta Lynn hair—
medium brunette, long and cut in layers that Tina styled in large,
bouncy curls. Her face was pleasant in a plain kind of way, but the
plain disappeared when Tina smiled. That's when Tina resembled
her daughter Charlotte the most. Tina must have been beautiful
when she was Charlotte's age, before life drained the pretty from
her features.

Charlotte was Jill's daughter's best friend. Jill had met Charlotte when both girls were nine. Charlotte had ridden the bus home
from school one afternoon with Emily. Charlotte had announced
to a surprised Jill that she was an accident that wasn't supposed to
happen, but that was okay because her mom loved her even if her
daddy didn't.

Charlotte's bluntness hadn't dimmed as she grew older. In a
way, Jill found it refreshing, but sometimes she wondered how
Tina put up with it on a constant basis.

"The girls get up okay this morning?" Jill asked. Emily had
spent the night at Charlotte's, giving Jill an unaccustomed quiet
morning at home by herself with no music blaring from Emily's
room.

Tina chuckled. "You should have heard them. All excited
about Homecoming. Making plans to go to the bonfire Friday
night, even talking about going to the game on Saturday before the
dance. You letting Emily go to that?"

Jill nodded. "It's all part of the high school experience."

Emily and Charlotte were high school freshmen. By the time
they got to be seniors, they might be too jaded to go to any Homecoming events—unless they were dating football players—but as
freshmen, high school was still new and fresh and exciting.

"Don't the seniors have beer at the bonfire?" Tina asked. "I
mean, they did back when I was in high school. Or... what I remember of high school anyway."

Jill had done the math a long time ago. Given her age, Tina

must have dropped out of high school before her senior year to have her daughter. Back in those days, pregnant students weren't allowed in the state's public schools.

Tina never said if she finished high school after Charlotte was born, and Jill didn't ask. She was one of the few people in Cumberland who knew that the boy who'd gotten Tina pregnant and then deserted her had robbed a convenience store in Reno a few months later and shot the clerk.

Last year he'd come back to Cumberland to get to know his daughter, he'd said. Jill had kept a close watch on him. So far he'd been a model citizen. Maybe he'd learned his lesson doing time at the state prison in Carson City. Jill hoped so.

"I'll have an officer or two on site at the school," Jill said. "There won't be any beer."

She had assigned an officer to patrol the bonfire every year since she'd taken office. The kids grumbled about it, and she'd even had a call from the football coach the first year. He hadn't come right out and said his boys resented not being able to drink at the bonfire, a long-standing tradition among the seniors, but the implication was clear.

Jill didn't care. Minors didn't drink in Silverado County if she could help it. Teenagers and alcohol didn't mix. Not that adults were much better, but at least she could do something about the kids. It made her vastly uncool among the high school kids, according to Emily. Jill didn't much care about that either.

Tina breathed a sigh of relief. "Good. Makes me feel a little better about letting Charlotte go. Don't want her making my mistakes, you know?" She scribbled something on her order pad, presumably Jill's normal breakfast order. "Be back with your meal in a few."

Jill poured herself a cup of tea and opened the morning edition of the *Silverado Gazette*. Nothing of local importance on the front page. Good. Maybe today would be an easy day.

When Jill opened the paper to page two, her own face stared back at her. She grimaced. She would never get used to seeing her campaign ads.

The November general election was the first in which Jill was officially running for sheriff. She'd been appointed to her post by the County Commissioners three years ago after Cory Fairmont retired.

Although she'd been Cory's chief deputy, she only got the job because Cory had thrown his considerable support behind her. Women might hold positions of power in boardrooms across the country, but in Silverado County the good old boy system still chugged right along. Men held all the important elected positions in the county—all except Jill's.

She'd spent the last three years making positive changes in the way things were done in the Sheriff's Department. The "no beer" policy at the bonfire was one. She'd instituted a zero tolerance policy for drunk drivers, no matter whose buddy they were.

She'd set also up the Secret Witness program that the County Commissioners didn't think was necessary and funded it by trimming overtime out of her office budget. She knew she was the right person for the job. She just had to convince the voters.

The election was a little less than four weeks away, and her own chief deputy was running against her. While Jill thought Oren Michaelson would make a good sheriff if the people elected him, she didn't want to lose.

Someone sat down around the corner of the counter while Jill was scanning the local section, looking for anything of interest. She lowered the paper.

"He's back again," Hal Taylor said without preamble. "Can't you do something about that?"

Jill didn't have to ask who was back or where he was. She'd had this conversation with Hal Taylor too many times to count.

The "he" was Jeremiah Corbitt, seventy years old and one of

Cumberland's crankiest senior citizens. Jeremiah was convinced that Hal, owner of Happy Hal's Cumberland Dodge, cheated him on a car repair job.

Most people would have written a few letters, maybe filed a complaint, and left it at that. Jeremiah Corbitt wasn't most people. When the letters didn't work, Jeremiah decided to stage his own one-man protest by picketing Hal's business.

In the grand scheme of things, a one-man picket line was little more than an annoyance. Except a persistent old man with a picket sign didn't make Happy Hal very happy, and an annoyed Hal Taylor was a thorn in Jill's side that she didn't need at seven-thirty in the morning.

Hal was the closest thing Cumberland had to a celebrity. He'd turned the one used car lot he'd inherited from his father into four new and used car dealerships. His goofy television commercials featuring Happy Hal and his sidekick, Hal's general manager Stan "Sad Sack" Schmidt, aired on the local television channels in both Cumberland and Reno more often than reality shows. Hal Taylor drew a lot of business to the area, and that made every business owner in Cumberland a Happy Hal fan.

Hal had been a senior in Cumberland High when Jill was a freshman, and the intervening decades had been kind to him. He hadn't been conventionally handsome back then, but he'd had more than enough charm to make up for it.

These days the lines around his mouth and creasing his forehead merely enhanced his rough features. His skin was a healthy tan year round. His black hair had gone salt and pepper in the way that made men look distinguished and women just look old. His shoulders were still broad like they'd been when he played football, and he hadn't let the rest of his muscles go to fat like so many former athletes did. He had a smile he could turn on at a moment's notice, and unlike many people who smiled for a living, Hal's smile reached and warmed his dark eyes. It was a good trait not only for a car salesman but for a politician, which probably explained why Hal was in his fourth term as County Commissioner.

In Cumberland, Hal Taylor had clout, and he wasn't above using it.

"Is Jeremiah on your property?" Jill asked Hal without closing the paper.

"He's at the Shell station across the street. Greg's not about to kick him off. He's got a soft spot for the old coot. I don't. He's not good for business."

Each time Hal complained, Jill sent out a deputy to roust Jeremiah, and each time Jeremiah promised to take his complaints to an attorney. Then a week or so later he'd show up again with another sign. He was smart enough never to set foot on Hal's property, so Jill couldn't arrest him for trespassing.

Unfortunately for Hal, the business owners where Jeremiah chose to picket, like Greg Seaborn who owned the Shell station across the street from Hal's Dodge dealership, saw him as harmless and let him wave his homemade picket signs at passing motorists to his heart's content.

"What, exactly, do you want me to do?" Jill asked. "He's not on your property, Greg's not going to kick him off his. Why can't you just fix his problem and send him away happy?"

Hal looked at her like she was a particularly disgusting form of insect life.

"Because we didn't cause his problem. I'm not about to start fixing—for free, mind you—every knock and ping in every ten-year-old Dodge in this valley, which is what will happen if I fix his car out of the goodness of my heart."

Tina interrupted them with Jill's breakfast. She filled Hal's coffee cup from the pot she carried in one hand.

"You having anything to eat this morning, Hal?" she asked.

Jill noticed that Tina smiled a little more for Hal, even put a little flirtatious lilt in her voice. Hal had that effect on women.

"No thanks, babe," Hal said, smiling back like he hadn't been annoyed just a moment ago. "Just coffee."

Hal's habit of calling women "babe" annoyed Jill, but Tina didn't seem to mind. She also didn't seem to mind that Hal was married. A plain gold wedding band was prominent on the ring finger of his left hand.

"If you change your mind, just let me know." Tina stuck her pad back in the deep front pocket of her apron and walked out into the diner proper, circulating among the tables and refilling coffee cups as she went.

"Cory would have done something," Hal said as he stirred a packet of sugar into his coffee. He didn't look at Jill. "So would Oren."

So far Hal hadn't endorsed Jill or Oren even though everyone knew Hal and Oren were long-time buddies. The whole campaign, outside of a few billboards and newspaper ads, had been rather low key. Apparently Hal thought he could manipulate Jill by threatening to throw his support behind her opponent.

"You sure you want to go there, Hal?" she said. "Over something like this?"

Jill had seen Hal throw his clout around during County Commission meetings, and she'd heard gossip that he'd used his influence and resources in much less savory ways as well. The gossip stopped short of actually accusing Hal of illegal activities, but Jill never forgot that Happy Hal had a darker side he didn't let the general public see.

"I just want to drive to work and not see him out in front of my business with those signs of his. It's bad for business, and it's bad for the town's image. Why can't you see that?"

Jill put her fork down on her plate. "Get a restraining order against him. He violates it, I'll arrest him."

"That would take too long."

It would also give Jeremiah his day in court, and the local

press would probably be there. Jeremiah with another protest sign didn't even merit a page five mention in the newspaper anymore, but Jeremiah going up against Happy Hal in court might even entice a news crew from Reno if they were having a slow news day.

"Look." Hal rubbed at his forehead. "Why don't you go talk to him? Your deputies go out and he gets his back up. You might have more luck with him. You're good with people, Jill, you always have been. Even when we were kids, you seemed to know how to connect with people."

Now he was flattering her. Pulling out all the big guns.

It never ceased to amaze her how in a town the size of Cumberland, small things became big things that had to be handled Right Now. Jeremiah Corbitt was clearly Hal Taylor's current big thing. Cory had warned Jill she'd have to play politics in this job. One of the people she had to play politics with was Hal Taylor. That didn't mean she had to like it.

Jill sighed and glanced at the neon-lit Coca-Cola clock on the back wall of the diner. The angle where she was sitting made it difficult to see precisely what time it was, but Jill could tell close enough. She didn't want to look at her watch; that was too obvious.

A mound of paperwork awaited her at her office, including the departmental budget report. She'd have just enough time to go talk to Jeremiah if she left soon.

"I'll go this one time," she said. "Next time, get a restraining order or I'm not sending anyone. Are we clear on that?"

Hal smiled, the same big grin he normally reserved for his television commercials. He thought he'd won, and maybe he had.

Jill didn't feel like she'd lost, though. Keeping the peace was her job. Talking to an angry old man was just one small part of it.

"Thanks, babe," Hal said. He finished the rest of his coffee, put a couple of dollar bills next to the empty cup, and stood up.

"Hal?" When he looked at her, Jill said, "Don't call me that. I prefer my name. I think you'll find most women do."

The look on his face said he didn't believe it. "You're okay, Jill." He gave her a mock salute with one finger and left the diner.

Great. She had the stamp of approval from Hal Taylor. Her day just couldn't get any better than that.

CHAPTER THREE

As soon as the door to the diner shut behind Jill, the aroma of bacon and fresh-out-of-the-oven biscuits was replaced by the smoky, outdoorsy scent of fields burned off after harvest and the snuffed-candle smell of diesel trucks passing by on Main. This morning the air also carried an almost indescribable scent of something else—that musty, early fall smell thick with the promise of winter rain and January snow.

Jill felt vaguely uneasy. Whether the feeling was the result of her conversation with Hal Taylor or from getting ready for work that morning in a quiet, teenager-free house, she had a ball of tension in her belly that left her with nervous energy and no outlet.

She'd parked her patrol car on a side street a block down from the diner. On her way back to the car, she bent over to pick up a crumpled-up brown paper bag from where it had blown against the base of one of the new golden locust trees that lined the sidewalks.

The mile-and-a-half section of Main the County Commissioners referred to as Cumberland's "downtown corridor" was in the midst of renovation, a plan spearheaded by Hal Taylor. Cobblestone walkways had replaced the cracked concrete sidewalks. Trees had been planted along the outside edge of the sidewalks, and covered trash receptacles were located on both sides of the street in every block. Old-fashioned wrought-iron benches had been bolted to the sidewalks in the shade of the trees, and near the center of town a circular, red brick roundabout separated the north and south-bound lanes of Main Street. Next spring a statue of a Pony Express rider would be installed in the center of the roundabout, and Jill had heard talk that a fountain would surround the base of the statue. Until the statute was ready, the roundabout held only a patch of lawn that was gradually turning brown in the cool fall nights and dry climate.

The renovation work gave downtown a quaint, old-fashioned, and slightly Victorian appeal. It reminded Jill of the way women dressed in the westerns her father had taken her to see on Saturday afternoons at the old Crest Theater. Prim and proper with their frilly lace parasols, the women in those movies never seemed touched by the dirt and dust of the Old West.

The Crest Theater was long gone, its balcony and lodge seating replaced with a four-plex of one large and three smaller theaters. A video game arcade had briefly flourished across the street from Cliff & Mattie's, but home video gaming systems had put it out of business. The empty storefront had been boarded over, and students from Cumberland High's art classes had designed and painted a mural on the flat boards that walled off the empty store. Cumberland's streets might not have been the packed-dirt wagon trails of old westerns, but the place still looked like it was caught suspended somewhere in its small town, Old West past.

Jill had almost reached her patrol car when her cell phone rang. She unclipped the cell from her belt and frowned as she saw the number of the sheriff's dispatch center on her display. Why would the dispatcher call her on her cell rather than the radio?

"What's going on?" she asked when she answered her phone.

"Didn't think you'd want this going out over the radio at the diner." Rachel, the day shift dispatcher, sounded stressed. "We've got a report of a body in that empty field at the end of Ponderosa next to Founder's Park."

A body. Jill took a deep breath, and the tension in her belly tightened. "What do we know?"

"Call came in on 9-1-1 a couple of minutes ago. A couple of scared kids, said their dog found a body when they were playing catch. Wouldn't give me their names, wouldn't stay on the line."

Jill unlocked her cruiser, got in, and buckled up. She didn't turn on the lights or the siren as she turned south on Main.

"Sounds like kids cutting school who didn't want to get caught," Jill said. "What else? They have any idea who it is?"

"They didn't say, just that it was a woman and there was a lot of blood. They couldn't see her face."

Most of Cumberland's transients stayed near the highway a mile or two out of town, hoping to catch a ride. Ponderosa Street was in a residential area a few miles west of the highway, close to where Cumberland proper gave way to the farmland and ranches that made up most of this part of Silverado County. Founders Park, with its baseball diamonds and picnic area, marked an unofficial delineation between the town and the ranches. Not a place Jill would normally expect to find someone just passing through. Even the tourists stuck close to Main Street. With Reno only sixty miles away, Cumberland wasn't exactly a destination spot, only a place to stop for gas and food, and maybe spend some time at the casino or in one of the local shops.

She didn't want to jump to conclusions. Her training told her not to, not until she had as many facts as she could gather. Still it was difficult not to wonder if the dead woman would turn out to be someone from town.

Someone Jill knew.

"Mason report in for duty yet?" she asked.

NEW PAGES

Mason Gibbons was a patrol deputy, one of a squad of ten who patrolled the entire expanse of Silverado County, five thousand square miles of mostly two-lane highways, dust, sagebrush, and the farming and ranching town of Cumberland. Mason had the most recent crime scene training among the deputies.

"He just left for patrol on 50 North," Rachel said.

Mason was also one of the best at catching speeders on the stretch of Highway 50 between Cumberland and Reno. Jill also had a zero-tolerance policy for speeders, something that definitely wasn't popular, but the speed limit was already seventy on parts of that highway. In a county that had as many free-range cattle as it had people, Jill thought seventy was fast enough.

"Call him back," Jill said. "I'll meet him at the scene. Call Howard Finneman. Get him out there, too."

"He's not on the roster today," Rachel said.

Jill knew Howard had requested the day off to drive his wife to Reno for a doctor's appointment. Betty Finneman had discovered a lump in her breast a week ago. Howard and Betty had been high school sweethearts. They'd celebrated their thirtieth wedding anniversary only last month. He might not be on the roster, but he was Jill's only forensic science officer. Whenever there was a dead body, Howard had to be there to supervise the scene and removal of the body.

"Tell Howard I'm sorry," Jill said. "Tell him..." She had been about to say tell him I don't have a choice, but Howard would already know that. "Tell him I'll meet him there. Tell him to call in whoever he needs to keep the crime scene secure."

Technically Jill could have done that, but she knew well enough to let her people do their jobs with as little interference from her as possible. Cory Fairmont had taught her that, and she'd always found it sound advice.

"Anything else?" Rachel asked. "What about Bradley?"

Bradley Winter was the editor and lone reporter for the Silverado Gazette. Bradley had a police scanner and a dearth of what he considered real local news to report.

"Make the calls you can on cell. Tell Howard and Mason to use radios only if they're out of cell range. If they have to use radios, keep it short and sweet. I don't want Bradley showing up until we know what we're dealing with."

"If he calls? Who do I refer him to?"

Strictly speaking, Oren as chief deputy was the department's press liaison. Since he'd announced he was running against Jill, she'd handled as much of the press contact as she could herself.

That didn't stop Bradley from contacting Oren on his own, but Jill wasn't about to give Oren any more free press than necessary.

"Tell him we'll have a statement for him as soon as we know anything."

Jill heard Rachel take a deep breath. Rachel had been on the job for only a year, had graduated from high school herself a scant five years earlier. She'd had some dispatcher experience in McGill, a small mining town near the Nevada/Utah border that made Cumberland look positively metropolitan by comparison. Rachel described McGill as being permanently stuck in the 50's, like something out of Mayberry RFD, a show that still aired there. No one had ever discovered a dead body in Mayberry.

"Rachel?" Jill said. "Relax. Handle it by the book. You know your job, and you're good at it. You made a good call, contacting me on the cell. You have any other concerns, you call me the same way."

Only after she'd thumbed off her cell phone did Jill remember Jeremiah Corbitt and his hand-lettered protest signs. She didn't have time now to persuade Jeremiah to try a different tactic with Hal Taylor. Depending on what she discovered in the field next to Founder's Park, she'd either go talk to him in an hour or two, or she'd call Rachel back and have her send out another deputy.

Jill turned right on Sycamore and drove past the south side of the high school. Ponderosa was the next left. Founder's Park was a mile south of the intersection of Ponderosa and Sycamore.

She could see the beginnings of the stack of wood for the bonfire in the high school parking lot. On Thursday night, the seniors on the football team would set fire to the wood scraps, dead tree branches, and other debris. A few flatbed trailers sat next to the pile of wood, ready for the kids to cover them in decorations for Saturday's Homecoming parade down Sycamore.

A school bus sat in the parking lot, the driver waiting for the last few kids to gather their backpacks. Students lingered around parked cars, some smoking, others with ear-bud wires trailing down to a pocket of their hoodie. Even after all these years, Jill could almost pick out the cliques—the jocks in their letterman jackets, the stoners in baggy clothes and dirty hair, the geeks dressed in clothes only their grandmothers would think fashionable, and the kids who sat on the student council dressed for high school success. She looked briefly for Emily and Charlotte but didn't see them.

Jill found herself wanting to pull into the parking lot, find her daughter, and just give her a hug. She needed some way to lessen the tension she felt, the same tension that made her grip the steering wheel too tightly and made her look at the kids in the parking lot a little too closely. A woman had died. She was somebody's daughter, maybe somebody's mother. Maybe even the mother of one of these kids.

Jill understood the loss of a parent. Her father had been killed when a drunk driver crossed the center line of Highway 50 and slammed into Charlie Jordon's patrol car. Her father had been killed instantly. Jill had been fifteen years old, the same age as Emily. Jill understood loss all too well.

She also understood her job. She was Emily's mom, but right now she was the sheriff, and she had a crime to investigate.

Jill turned off Sycamore onto Ponderosa and headed toward Founder's Park, leaving the high school—and Emily—behind.

A Death
in
Cumberland

is available in paperback and

in all e-book formats

ABOUT THE AUTHOR

ANNIE REED describes herself as a desert rat who longs to live by the ocean. Born and raised in Nevada, Annie started her career in science fiction. She soon branched out to fantasy, mystery, and crime fiction, as well as a number of mainstream stories featuring what Annie describes as "sturdy, middle-aged women," perhaps, she says, because she happens to be one herself.

No matter what genre, the hallmark of Annie's writing has always been the strong, relatable, and memorable characters who populate her fiction.

Annie still lives in Northern Nevada with her husband and daughter, who share their house with a number of high-maintenance cats. A friend to backyard bunnies and kamikaze quail, Annie would probably befriend dogs, too, except they'd chase the rabbits.

To find out more about Annie, visit www.annie-reed.com.